John Kendrick Bangs

# The Booming of Acre Hill

John Kendrick Bangs

# The Booming of Acre Hill

1st Edition | ISBN: 978-3-73409-309-8

Place of Publication: Frankfurt am Main, Germany

Year of Publication: 2019

Outlook Verlag GmbH, Germany.

Reproduction of the original.

# THE BOOMING OF ACRE HILL

*and Other Reminiscences of Urban and Suburban Life*

# The Booming of Acre Hill

By

## John Kendrick Bangs

Illustrated By C. Dana Gibson
Published in New York and London, 1902.

TO
WILLIAM LIVERMOREKINGMAN,
WITH AFFECTIONATE REGARDS

These stories by Mr. Bangs have appeared from time to time in *The Ladies Home Journal, The Woman's Home Companion*, and the various publications of Messrs. HARPER & BROTHERS.

# CONTENTS

THE BOOMING OF ACRE HILL
THE STRANGE MISADVENTURES OF AN ORGAN
THE PLOT THAT FAILED
THE BASE INGRATITUDE OF BARKIS, M.D.
THE UTILITARIAN MR. CARRAWAY
THE BOOK SALES OF MR. PETERS
THE VALOR OF BRINLEY
WILKINS
**THE MAYOR'S LAMPS**
THE BALANCE OF POWER
**JARLEY'S EXPERIMENT**
**JARLEY'S THANKSGIVING**
HARRY AND MAUDE AND I—ALSO JAMES
AN AFFINITIVE ROMANCE

    I. MR. AUGUSTUS RICHARDS'S IDEAL
    II. MISS HENDERSON'S STANDARD
    III. A GLANCE AT MISS FLORA HENDERSON HERSELF
    IV. A BRIEF GLIMPSE OF MR. AUGUSTUS RICHARDS
    V. CONCLUSION

**MRS. UPTON'S DEVICE**

    I. THE RESOLVE
    II. A SUCCESSFUL CASE
    III. A SET-BACK
    IV. THE DEVICE

# ILLUSTRATIONS

"I'LL NEVER, NEVER, NEVER, SO LONG AS I LIVE"
DURING THE INTERMEZZO

# THE BOOMING OF ACRE HILL

Acre Hill ten years ago was as void of houses as the primeval forest. Indeed, in many ways it suggested the primeval forest. Then the Acre Hill Land Improvement Company sprang up in a night, and before the bewildered owners of its lovely solitudes and restful glades, who had been paying taxes on their property for many years, quite grasped the situation they found that they had sold out, and that their old-time paradise was as surely lost to them as was Eden to Adam and Eve.

To-day Acre Hill is gridironed with macadamized streets that are lined with houses of an architecture of various degrees of badness. Where birds once sang, and squirrels gambolled, and stray foxes lurked, the morning hours are made musical by the voices of milkmen, and the squirrels have given place to children and nurse-maids. Where sturdy oaks stood like sentinels guarding the forest folk from intrusion from the outside world now stand tall wooden poles with glaring white electric lights streaming from their tops. And the soughing of the winds in the trees has given place to the clang of the bounding trolley. All this is the work of the Acre Hill Land Improvement Company.

Yet if, as I have said, the Acre Hill Land Improvement Company sprang up in a night, it passed many sleepless nights before it received the rewards which come to him who destroys Nature. And when I speak of a corporation passing sleepless nights I do so advisedly, for at the beginning of its career the Acre Hill Land Improvement Company consisted of one man—a mild-mannered man who had previously labored in similar enterprises, and whose name was called blessed in a thousand uncomfortable houses in uncomfortable suburbs elsewhere, that, like Acre Hill, had once been garden spots, but had been "improved." Even a professional improver of land finds sleep difficult to woo at the beginning of such an enterprise. In the first instance, when one buys land, giving a mortgage in full payment therefor, with the land as security, one appears to have assumed a moderately heavy burden. Then, when to this one adds the enormous expense of cutting streets through the most beautiful of the sylvan glades, the building of sewers, and the erection of sample houses, to say nothing of the strain upon the intellect in the selection of names for the streets and lanes and circles that spring into being, one cannot but wonder how the master mind behind it all manages to survive.

But the Acre Hill Land Improvement Company did survive, and Dumfries

Corners watched its progress with much interest. Regrets were expressed when some historic knoll was levelled in order to provide a nice flat space for a public square. Youngsters who had bagged many a partridge on Acre Hill felt like weeping when one stretch of bush after another was cut ruthlessly away in order that a pretentious-looking structure, the new home of the Acre Hill Country Club, might be erected. Lovers sighed when certain noble old oaks fraught with sentimental associations fell before the unsentimental axes of the Improvement Company; and numberless young Waltons muttered imprecations upon the corporation that filled in with stone and ashes the dear old pond that once gave forth fish in great abundance, and through earthen pipes diverted the running brook, that hitherto had kept it full, into a brand-new sewer.

These lovers of nature could not understand the great need of our constantly growing population for uncomfortable houses in inconvenient suburbs, and in their failure to comprehend they became cavilers. But others —those who admire the genius which enables a man to make unproductive land productive, who hail as benefactor one who supplants a profitless oak of a thousand years' standing with a thriving butcher-shop—these people understood what was being done for Dumfries Corners, but wondered how the venture was to be made profitable. There were already more vacant houses in Dumfries Corners than could be rented, more butcher-shops than could be supported, more clubs than could be run without a deficit. But the Acre Hill Land Improvement Company went on, and within three years paradise had become earth, and the mild-mannered and exceedingly amiable gentleman who had replaced the homes of the birds with some fifteen or twenty houses for small families could look about him and see greater results than ever greeted the eyes of Romulus in the days of the great Rome Land Improvement Company.

Most wonderful of all, he was still solvent! But a city is not a city, nor, in its own degree, a suburb a suburb, without inhabitants; and while to a mind like that back of the Acre Hill Land Improvement Company it is seemingly a moderately easy task to lay out a suburb in so far as its exterior appointments are concerned, the rub comes in the getting of citizens. A Standard Oil magnate can build a city if he is willing to spend the money, but all the powers of heaven and earth combined cannot manufacture offhand a citizenship. In an emergency of this nature most land improvement companies would have issued pretty little pamphlets, gotten up in exquisite taste, full of beautiful pictures and bubbling over with enthusiastic text, all based upon possibilities rather than upon realities.

But the Acre Hill Land Improvement Company was sincere and honest. It believed in advertising what it had; it believed in dilating somewhat on the possibilities, but it was too honest to claim for itself virtues it did not possess.

So it tried different methods. The Acre Hill Country Club was the first of these, and a good idea it was. It was successful from the start, socially. Great numbers attended the entertainments and dances, although these were rather poorly conducted. Still, the Country Club was a grand success. It gave much and received nothing. Dumfries Corners, reluctant to approve of anything, approved of it.

But no lots were sold! The Acre Hill Land Improvement Company was willing to make itself popular—very willing. Didn't mind giving Dumfries Corners people free entertainment, but—lots didn't sell. What is the use of paying the expenses of a club if lots don't sell? This was a new problem for the company to consider. There were sixteen houses ready for occupancy, and consuming interest at a terrible rate, but no one came to look at them. Acre Hill was a charming spot, no doubt, but for some unknown reason or other it failed to take hold of the popular fancy, despite the attractions of the club.

Suddenly the head of the institution had an idea. In the great metropolis there was an impecunious and popular member of Uppertendom whose name had been appearing in the society journals with great frequency for years. He formerly had been prosperous, but now he was down financially; yet society still received and liked him, for he had many good points and was fundamentally what the world calls a good fellow.

"Why not send for Jocular Jimson Jones?" suggested the head and leading spirit of the Improvement Company. "We can offer him one of our cottages, and pay his debts if he has any, if he will live here and give us the benefit of his social prestige."

The suggestion was received with enthusiasm. Mr. Jones was summoned, came and inspected the cottage, and declined. He really couldn't, you know. Of course he was down, but not quite down to the level of a cottage of that particular kind. He still had plenty of friends whom he could visit and who would be charmed to entertain him in the style to which he was accustomed. Why, therefore, should he do this thing, and bring himself down to the level of the ordinary commuter? No, indeed. Not he! The Directors saw the point, and next offered him—and this time he accepted—the free use of the residence of one of the officers of the company, a really handsome, pretentious structure, with a commanding view, stable, green-houses, graceful lawns, and all other appurtenances of a well-appointed country seat. In addition to the furnishing of the house in proper taste, they put coal in the cellar and fly-screens in the windows. They filled the residence with servants, and indorsed the young person at the grocer's and butcher's. They bought him a surrey and a depot wagon. They bought him horses and they stocked him well with fine cigars. They paid his tailor's bills, and sundry other pressing monetary affairs were funded. In fact, the Acre Hill Land Improvement Company set Jocular Jimson Jones up and then gave him *carte blanche* to entertain; and inasmuch as Jocular had a genius for entertaining, it is hardly necessary to say that he availed himself of his opportunity.

During that first summer at Acre Hill Mr. Jones had the best time of his life. His days were what the vulgar term "all velvet." His new residence was so superb that it restored his credit in the metropolis, and city "swells," to whom he was under social obligation, went home, after having been paid in kind, wondering if Jocular Jimson Jones had unearthed somewhere a recently deceased rich uncle. He gave suppers of most lavish sort. He had vaudeville shows at the club-house, with talent made up of the most exclusive young men and women of the city. The Amateur Thespians of the Borough of Manhattan gave a whole series of performances at the club during the autumn, and by slow degrees the society papers began to take notice. Acre Hill began to be known as "a favorite resort of the 400." Nay, even the sacred 150 had penetrated to its very core, wonderingly, however, for none knew how Jocular Jimson Jones could do it. Still, they never declined an invitation. As a natural result the market for Acre Hill lots grew active. The sixteen cottages were sold, and the purchasers found themselves right in the swim. It was the easiest thing in the world to get into society if you only knew how. Jocular Jimson Jones was a fine, approachable, neighborly person, and at the Country Club dances was quite as attentive to the hitherto unknown Mrs. Scraggs as he was to Mrs. John Jacob Wintergreen, the acknowledged leader of the 400. Mrs. Wintergreen, too, was not unapproachable. She talked pleasantly during a musicale at the club-house with Mr. Scraggs, and said she hoped some day to have the pleasure of meeting Mrs. Scraggs; and when Scraggs, in response, said he would go and get her she most amiably begged him not to leave her alone.

Months went by, and where sixteen empty houses had been, there were now sixty all occupied, and lots were going like hot cakes. Tuxedo was in the shade. Lenox was dying. Newport was dead. Society flocked to Acre Hill and hobnobbed with Acre Hillians. Acre Hillians became somewhat proud of themselves, and rather took to looking down upon Dumfries Corners people. Dumfries Corners people were nice, and all that, but not particularly interesting in the sense that "our set," with Jocular Jimson Jones at the head of it, was interesting.

Then came the County Ball. This Jocular engineered himself, and the names of the lady patrons were selected from the oldest and the newest on the list. Mrs. Wintergreen's name led, of course, but Mrs. Scraggs' name was there too, sandwiched in between those of Mrs. Van Cortlandtuyvel and Mrs. Gardenior, of Gardenior's Island, representing two families which would carry social weight either in Boston or the "other side of Market Street." There were four exalted names from the city, one from Dumfries Corners, and seven from Acre Hill.

Then more lots sold, and still more, and then, alas, came the end! Jocular Jimson Jones was too successful.

After two years of glory the social light of Acre Hill went out. The Acre Hill Land Improvement Company retired from the business. All its lots were sold, and, of course, there was no further need for the services of Jocular Jimson Jones. His efforts were crowned with success. His mission was accomplished, but he moved away—I think regretfully, for, after all, he had found the Acre Hill people a most likable lot—but it was inevitable that, there being no more fish to catch, the anglers needed no bait, and Jocular Jimson had to go. Where he has gone to there is no one who knows. He has disappeared wholly, even in the metropolis, and, most unfortunately for Acre Hill, with Jocular Jimson Jones have departed also all its social glories. None of the elect come to its dances any more. The amateur thespians of the exclusive set no longer play on the stage of its club-house, and it was only last week that Mrs. John Jacob Wintergreen passed Mr. Scraggs on the street with a cold glare of unrecognition.

Possibly when Acre Hill reads this it will understand, possibly not.

Dumfries Corners people understood it right along, but then they always were a most suspicious lot, and fond of an amusing spectacle that cost them nothing.

# THE STRANGE MISADVENTURES OF AN ORGAN

Carson was a philosopher, and on the whole it was a great blessing that he was so. No man needed to be possessor of a philosophical temperament more than he, for, in addition to being a resident of Dumfries Corners, Carson had other troubles which, to an excitable nature, would have made life a prolonged period of misery. He was the sort of a man to whom irritating misfortunes of the mosquito order have a way of coming. To some of us it seemed as if a spiteful Nature took pleasure in pelting Carson with petty annoyances, none of them large enough to excite compassion, many of them of a sort to provoke a quiet smile. Of all the dogs in the neighborhood it was always his dog that got run into the pound, although it was equally true that Carson's dog was one of the few that were properly licensed. If he bought a new horse something would happen to it before a week had elapsed; and how his coachman once ripped off the top of his depot wagon by driving it under a loose telephone wire is still one of the stories of the vicinity in which he lives. Anything out of the way in the shape of trouble seemed to choose the Carson household for experimental purposes. He was the medium by which new varieties of irritations were introduced to an ungrateful world, but such was his nature that, given the companionship of Herbert Spencer and a cigar, he could be absolutely counted on not to murmur.

This disposition to accept the trials and tribulations which came upon him without a passionate outburst was not by any means due to amiability. Carson was of too strong a character to be continually amiable. He merely exercised his philosophy in meeting trouble. He boiled within, but presented a calm, unruffled front to the world, simply because to do otherwise would involve an expenditure of nervous force which he did not consider to be worth while.

I can never forget the sense of admiring regard which I experienced when in Genoa, while he and I were about to enter our banker's together, he slipped upon a bit of banana peeling, bruising his knee and destroying his trouser leg. I should have indulged in profane allusions to the person who had thoughtlessly thrown the peeling upon the ground if by some mischance the accident had happened to me. Carson, however, did nothing of the sort, but treated me to a forcible abstract consideration of the unthinking habits of the masses.

The unknown individual who was responsible for the accident did not enter into the question; no one was consigned to everlasting torture in the deepest depths of purgatory; a calm, dispassionate presentation of an abstraction was all that greeted my ears. The practice of thoughtlessness was condemned as a thing entirely apart from the practitioner, and as a tendency needing correction. Inwardly, I know he swore; outwardly, he was as serene as though nothing untoward had happened to him. It was then that I came to admire Carson. Before that he had my affectionate regard in fullest measure, but now admiration for his deeper qualities set in, and it has in no sense diminished as time has passed. Once, and once only, have I known him to depart from his philosophical demeanor, and that one departure was, I think, justified by the situation, since it was the culminating point of a series of aggravations, to fail to yield to which would have required a more than human strength.

The incident to which I refer was in connection with a fine organ, which at large expense Carson had had built in his house, for, like all philosophers, Carson has a great fondness for music, and is himself a musician of no mean capacity. I have known him to sit down under a parlor-lamp and read over the score of the "Meistersinger" just as easily as you or I would peruse one of the lighter novels of the day. This was one of his refuges. When his spirit was subjected to an extreme tension he relieved his soul by flying to the composers; to use his own very bad joke, when he was in need of composure he sought out the "composures." As time progressed, however, and the petty annoyances grew more numerous, the merely intellectual pleasure of the writings of Wagner and Handel and Mozart possibly failed to suffice, and an organ was contracted for.

"I enjoy reading the music," said he as we sat and talked over his plan, "but sometimes—very often, in fact—I feel as if something ought to shriek, and I'm going to have an organ of my own to do it for me."

So, as I have said, the organ was contracted for, was built, and an additional series of trials began. Upon a very important occasion the organ declined to shriek, although every effort to persuade it to perform the functions for which it was designed was made. Forty or fifty very charming people were gathered together to be introduced to the virtues of the new instrument—for Carson was not the kind of man to keep to himself the good things which came into his life; he shared all his blessings, while keeping his woes to himself; a well-known virtuoso was retained to set forth the possibilities of the acquisition, and all was going as "merry as a marriage bell" when suddenly there came a wheeze, and the fingers of the well-known virtuoso were powerless to elicit the harmonious shrieks which all had come to hear.

It was a sad moment, but Carson was equal to the occasion.

"Something's out of gear," he said, with a laugh due rather to his philosophical nature than to mirth. "I'm afraid we'll have to finish on the piano."

And so we did, and a delightful evening we had of it, although many of us went home wondering what on earth was the matter with the organ.

A few days later I met Carson on the train and the mystery was solved.

"The trouble was with the water-pipes," he explained. "They were put in wrong, and the location of the house is such that every time Colonel Hawkins, on the other side of the street, takes a bath, all the water that flows down the hill is diverted into his tub."

I tried not to laugh.

"You'll have to enter into an agreement with the Colonel," I said. "Make him promise not to bathe between certain hours."

"That's a good idea," said Carson, smiling, "but after all I guess I'd better change the pipes. Heaven forbid that in days like these I should seek to let any personal gratification stand between another man and the rare virtue of cleanliness."

Several weeks went by, and men were busily employed in seeing that the water supply needed for a proper running of the organ came direct from the mains, instead of coming from a pipe of limited capacity used in common by a half dozen or more residents of a neighboring side street.

Somewhere about the end of the fourth week Carson invited me to dinner. The organ was all right again, he said. The water supply was sufficient, and if I cared to I might dine with him, and afterward spend an evening sitting upon the organ bench while Carson himself manipulated the keys. I naturally accepted the invitation, since, in addition to his other delightful qualities, Carson is a past grand-master in the art of giving dinners. He is a man with a taste, and a dinner good enough for him is a thing to arouse the envy of the gods. Furthermore, as I have already said, he is a musician of no mean order, and I know of no greater pleasure than that of sitting by his side while he "potters through a score," as he puts it. But there was a disappointment in store for us. I called at the appointed hour and found the household more or less in consternation. The cook had left, and a dinner of "cold things" confronted us.

"She couldn't stand the organ," explained Carson. "She said it got on to her nerves—'rumblin' like.'"

I gazed upon him in silent sympathy as we dined on cold roast beef, stuffed olives, and ice cream.

"This is serious," my host observed as we sat over our coffee and cigars after the repast. "That woman was the only decent cook we've managed to secure in seven years, and, by Jingo, the minute she gets on to my taste the organ gets on to her nerves and she departs!"

"One must eat," I observed.

"That's just it," said Carson. "If it comes to a question of cook or organ the organ will have to go. She was right about it, though. The organ does rumble like the dickens. Some of the bass notes make the house buzz like an ocean-steamer blowing off steam."

It was a picturesque description, for I had noticed at times that when the organ was being made to shriek fortissimo every bit of panelling in the house seemed to rattle, and if a huge boiler of some sort suffering from internal disturbance had been growling down in the cellar, the result would have been quite similar.

"It may work out all right in time," Carson said. "The thing is new yet, and you can't expect it to be mellow all at once. What I'm afraid of, apart from the inability of our cook to stand the racket, is that this quivering will structurally weaken the house. What do you think?"

"Oh, I don't know," I said. "Some of the wainscot panels rattle a bit, but I imagine the house will stand it unless you go in too much for Wagner. 'Tannhäuser' or 'Siegfried' might shake a few beams loose, but lighter music, I think, can be indulged in with impunity."

Time did not serve, as Carson had hoped, to mellow things. Indeed, the succeeding weeks brought more trouble, and most of it came through the organ. Some of the rattling panels, in spite of every effort to make them fast, rattled the more. One night when the servants were alone in the house, of its own volition the organ sent forth, to break the still hours, a blood-curdling basso-profundo groan that suggested ghosts to their superstitious minds. The housemaid came to regard the instrument as something uncanny, and, even as the cook had done before her, shook the dust of the house of Carson from her feet.

Then a rat crawled into one of the pipes—Carson was unable to ascertain which—and died there, with results that baffle description. I doubt if Wagner himself could have expressed the situation in his most inspired moments. Still Carson was philosophical.

"I'll play a requiem to the rodent," he said, "that will make him turn over in his grave, wherever that interesting spot may be."

This he did, and the effect was superb, and no doubt the deceased did turn over in his grave, for the improvisation called into play every pipe on the whole instrument. However, I could see that this constant pelting at the hands of an unkind fate through the medium of his most cherished possession was having its effect upon Carson's hitherto impregnable philosophy. When he spoke of the organ it was with a tone of suppressed irritation which boded ill, and finally I was not surprised to hear that he had offered to give the organ away.

"After all," he said, "I made a mistake—flying so high. A man doesn't want a church-organ in his house any more than he wants an elephant for a lap-dog. I've offered it to the Unitarian Church."

I felt a little hurt about this, for my own church was badly in need of an instrument of that nature, but I said nothing, and considering the amount of trouble the organ had given I got over my regret when I realized that the Unitarian Church, and not mine, was shortly to have it. In this, however, I was mistaken, for, after due deliberation, the Unitarians decided that the organ was so very large that they'd have to build a new church to go with it, and so declined it with thanks.

Carson bit his lip and then offered it to us. "Don't seem to be able to give it away," he said. "But I'll try again. You tell your vestry that if they want it they can have it. I'll take it out and put it in the barn up in the hay-loft. They can take it or leave it. It will cost them cartage and the expense of putting it up."

I thanked him, and joyously referred the matter to the vestry. At first the members of that body were as pleased as I was, but after a few minutes of jubilation the Chairman of the Finance Committee asked; "How much will it cost to get this thing into shape?"

Nobody knew, and finally the acceptance of the gift was referred to a committee consisting of the Chairman of the Finance Committee, the Chairman of the Music Committee, and myself, with full power to act.

Inquiry showed that the cost of every item in connection with the acceptance of the gift would amount to about a thousand dollars, and we called upon Carson to complete the arrangement. He received us cordially. We thanked him for his generosity, and were about to accept the gift finally, when the Chairman of the Finance Committee said:

"It is very good of you, Mr. Carson, to give us this organ. Heaven knows we need it, but it will cost us about a thousand dollars to put it in."

"So I judged," said Carson. "But when it is in you'll have a thirty-five-hundred-dollar organ."

"Splendid!" ejaculated the Chairman of the Music Committee.

"The great difficulty that now confronts us," said the financier, "is as to how we shall raise that money. The church is very poor."

"I presume it is a good deal of a problem in these times," acquiesced Carson. "Ah—"

"It's a most baffling one," continued the financier. "I suppose, Mr. Carson," he added, "that if we do put it in and pass around a subscription paper, we can count on you for—say two hundred and fifty dollars?"

I stood aghast, for I saw the thread of Carson's philosophy snap.

"What?" he said, with an effort to control himself.

"I say I suppose we can count on you for a subscription of two hundred and fifty dollars," repeated the financier.

There was a pause that seemed an eternity in passing. Carson's face worked convulsively, and the seeming complacency of the Chairman of the Finance Committee gave place to nervous apprehension as he watched the color surge through the cheeks and temples of our host.

He thought Carson was about to have a stroke of apoplexy.

I tried to think of something to say that might relieve the strain, but it wouldn't come, and on the whole I rather enjoyed the spectacle of the strong philosopher struggling with inclination, and I think the philosopher might have conquered had not the Chairman of the Music Committee broken in jocularly with:

"Unless he chooses to make it five hundred dollars, eh?" And he grinned maddeningly as he added: "If you'll give five hundred dollars we'll put a brass plate on it and call it 'The Carson Memorial,' eh? Ha—ha—ha."

Carson rose from his seat, walked into the hall and put on his hat. "Mr.—

ah—Blank," said he to the financier, "would you and Mr. Hicks mind walking down to the church with me?"

"Say, he's going to put it in for us!" whispered Hicks, the Chairman of the Music Committee, rubbing his hands gleefully.

"Don't you want me, Carson?" I asked, rising.

"No—you stay here!" he replied, shortly.

And then the three went out, while I lit a cigar and pottered about Carson's library. In half an hour he returned alone. His face was red and his hand trembled slightly, but otherwise he had regained his composure.

"Well?" said I.

"Well, I'm going to put it up," said he.

"Now—see here, Carson," I remonstrated. It seemed so like a rank imposition on his generosity. To give the organ was enough, without putting him to the expense of erecting it.

"Don't interrupt," said he. "I'm not going to put it up in the organ-loft, as you suppose, but in a place where it is likely to be quite as much appreciated."

"And that?" I asked.

"In the hay-loft," he replied.

"I don't blame you," said I, after a pause.

"Neither do I," said he.

"But why did you go down to the church?" I asked.

"Well," he explained, chuckling in spite of himself. "It was this way. My grandfather, I have been told, used to be able to express himself profanely without using a profane word, but I can't, and there were one or two things I wanted to say to those men that wouldn't go well with the decorations of my house, and which couldn't very well be said to a guest in my house."

"But, man alive, you didn't go to the church to do your swearing?"

"No," he answered. "I did it on the way down; and," he added, enthusiastically, "I did it exceeding well."

"But why the church?" I persisted.

"I thought after what I had to say to them," said he, "that they might need a little religious consolation."

And with that the subject was dropped.

The organ, as Carson threatened, was transferred to the hay-loft and not to the church, and as for the two Chairmen, they have several times expressed themselves to the effect that Carson is a very irritable, not to say profane, person.

But I am still inclined to think him a philosopher. Under the provocation any man of a less philosophical temperament might have forgotten the laws of hospitality and cursed his offending guests in his own house.

# THE PLOT THAT FAILED

Among the most promising residents of Dumfries Corners some ten years ago was a certain Mr. Richard Partington Smithers, whose brilliant début and equally sudden extinguishment in the field of literary endeavor have given rise from time to time to no little discussion. He was young, very young, indeed, at the time of his great literary success, and his friends and neighbors prophesied great things for him. Yet nothing has since come from his pen, and many have wondered why.

Thanks to Mr. Smithers himself I am enabled to make public the story of his sudden withdrawal from the ranks of the immortals when on the very threshold of the temple of fame.

Ten years have changed his point of view materially, and an experience that once seemed tragedy to him is now in his eyes sufficiently tinged with comedy, and his own position among us is so secure that he is willing that the story of his failure should go forth.

After trying many professions Smithers had become a man of schemes. He devised plans that should enrich other people. Unfortunately, he sold these to other people on a royalty basis, and so failed to grow rich himself. If he had only sold his plans outright and collected on the spot he might sometime have made something; but this he did not do, and as a consequence he rarely made anything that was at all considerable, and finally, to keep the wolf out of his dining-room, he was forced to take up poetry, that being in his estimation the last as well as the easiest resource of a well-ordered citizen.

"I always threatened to take up poetry when all else had failed me," he said to himself; "therefore I will now proceed to take up poetry. Writing is purely manual labor, anyhow. Given a pad, a pencil, and perseverance—three very important p's—and I can produce a fourth, a poem, in short order. Sorry I didn't get to the end of my other ropes before, now that I think of it."

And so he sat down and took up poetry.

He put it down again, however, very quickly.

"Dear me!" he ejaculated. "Now, who'd have thought that? Here I have the pencil and the pad and the perseverance, but I'm hanged if the poem is quite as easy as I had supposed. These little conceits aren't so easy to write, after all, even when they contain no ideas. Of course, it isn't hard to say:

"'Sweet month of May, time of the violet wild,
The dandelion golden, and the mild
Ethereal sweetness of the blossoming trees,
The soft suggested calor of the breeze,
The ruby-breasted robin on the lawn,
The thrushes piping sweetly at the dawn,
The gently splashing waters by the weir,
The rose- and lilac-laden atmosphere'—

"because, after all, it's nothing but a catalogue of the specialties of May;
but how the dickens to wind the thing up is what puzzles me. It's too beautiful
and truly poetic to be spoiled by a completing couplet like:

"'And in the distant dam the croaking frog
Completes, O May, thy wondrous catalogue.'

"Nobody would take a thing like that—and pay for it; but what else can be
said? What do the violets wild, the dandelion, the ruby-breasted robin, and the
lilac-laden atmosphere and other features all do, I'd like to know? What one
of many verbs—oh, tut! Poetry very evidently is not in my line, after all. I'll
turn the vials of my vocabulary upon essay-writing."

Which Partington, as his friends called him, proceeded at once to do. He
applied himself closely to his desk for one whole morning, and wrote a very
long paper on "The Tendency of the Middle Ages Towards Artificialism."
Hardly one of the fifteen thousand words employed by him in the
construction of this paper held fewer than five syllables, and one or two of
them got up as high as ten, a fact which led Partington to think that the editor
of the *South American Quarterly Review* ought at least to have the refusal of
it. Apparently the editor of the *South American Quarterly Review* was only
too eager to have the refusal of it, because he refused it, or so Partington
observed in confidence to an acquaintance, in less time than it could possibly
have taken him to read it. After that the essay became emulous of men like
Stanley and Joe Cook. It became a great traveller, but never failed to get back
in safety to its fond parent, Richard Partington Smithers, as our hero now
called himself. Finally, Partington did manage to realize something on his
essay—that is to say, indirectly—for after "The Tendency of the Middle Ages
Towards Artificialism" had gone the rounds of all the reviews, monthlies,
dailies, and weeklies in the country, its author pigeon-holed it, and, stringing
together the printed slips it had brought back to him upon the various
occasions of its return, he sent these under the head of "How Editors Reject"
to an evening journal in Boston, whose readers could know nothing of the
subject, for reasons that are familiar to those who are acquainted with
American letters. For this he not only received the editor's thanks, but a six

months' subscription to the journal in question—the latter of which was useful, since every night, excluding Sundays, its columns contained much valuable information on such subjects as "How to Live on Fifty Dollars a Year," "How to Knit an Afghan with One Needle," and "How Not to Become a Novelist."

Discouraged by the fate of his essay, Partington endeavored to get a position on a railway somewhere as a conductor or brakeman; but failing in this, he returned once more to his writing-table and wrote a novel. This was the hardest work he had ever attempted. It took him quite a week to think his story out and put it together; but when he had it done he was glad he had stuck conscientiously to it, for the results really seemed good to him. The book was charmingly written, he thought; so charming, in fact, that he did not think it necessary to have a type-written copy made of it before sending it out to the publishers. Possibly this was a mistake. For a time Partington really believed it was a mistake, because the publisher who saw it first returned it without comment, prejudiced against it, no doubt, by the fact that it came to him in the author's autograph. The second publisher was not so rude. He said he would print it if Partington would advance one thousand dollars to protect him against loss. The third publisher evidently thought better of the book, for he only demanded protection to the amount of seven hundred and fifty dollars, which, of course, Partington could not pay; and in consequence *False but Fair* never saw the light of day as a published book.

"Is it rejected because of its length, its breadth, or what?" he had asked the last publisher who had turned his back on the book.

"Well, to tell you the truth, Mr. Smithers," the publisher had answered, "all that our readers had to say about it—and the three who read it agreed unanimously—was that the book is immature. You do not write like an adult."

"Thanks," said Partington, as he bowed himself out. "If that's the truth, I'll try writing for juveniles. I'll sit right down to-night and knock off a short story about 'Tommy and the Huckleberry-tree.' I don't know whether huckleberries grow on trees or on huckles, but that will make the tale all the more interesting. If they don't grow on trees people will regard the story as romance. If they do grow on trees it will be realism."

True to his promise, that night Partington did write a story, and it was, as he had said it should be, about "Tommy and the Huckleberry-tree"; and so amusing did it appear to the editor of that eminent juvenile periodical, *Nursery Days*, because of what he supposed was the author's studied ignorance on the subject of huckleberries, that it was accepted instanter, and the name of Richard Partington Smithers shortly appeared in all the glory of type.

Partington walked on air for at least a week after his effusion appeared in print. He had visions night and day in which he seemed to see himself the centre of the literary circle, and as he promenaded the avenue in the afternoons he felt almost inclined to stop people who passed him by to tell them who he was, and thus enable them to feast their eyes on one whose name would shortly become a household word. All reasonable young authors feel this way after their first draught at the soul-satisfying spring of publicity. It is only that preposterous young person who was born tired who fails to experience the sensations that were Partington's that week; and at the end of the week, again like the reasonable young author, he began to realize that immortality could not be gained by one story treating of a fictitious Tommy and an imaginary huckleberry-tree, and so he sat himself down at his desk once more, resolved this time to clinch himself, as it were, in the public mind, with a tale of "Jimmie and the Strawberry-mine." This story did not come as easily as the other. In fact, Partington found it impossible to write more than a third of the second tale that night. He couldn't bring his mind down to it exactly, probably because his mind had been soaring so high since the publication of his first effusion. For diversion as much as for anything else during a lull in his flow of language he penned a short letter to the editor of *Nursery Days*, and announced his intention to send the story of "Jimmie and the Strawberry-mine" to him shortly—which was unfortunate. If he had finished the story first and then sent it, it might have been good enough to convince the editor against his judgment that he ought to have it. A concrete story can often accomplish more than an abstract idea. In this event it could not have accomplished less, anyhow, for the editor promptly replied that he did not care for a second story of that nature. There was no particular evidence in hand, he said, that the children liked stories of that kind particularly, adding that the first was only an experiment that it was not necessary to repeat, and so on; polite, but unmistakably valedictory.

"No evidence in hand that they are liked, eh? Well, how on earth, I wonder," Partington said, angrily, to himself, "do they ever find evidence that things are liked? Do they go about asking subscribers, or what?"

And then he picked up the issue of *Nursery Days* that had started him along on his way to immortality, to console himself, at all events, with the sight of his published story. In turning over the leaves of the periodical his eye fell upon a page across the top of which ran a highly ornate cut which indicated that there was printed the "Post-office Department of *Nursery Days*," on perusing which Partington found a number of communications and editorial responses like these:

**I.**

"DEAR POSTMASTER,—I have been taking *Nursery Days* since Christmas, so I thought I would write you a letter. My birthday came a week ago Thursday. I received a watch and chain, a glove-buttoner, a penknife, and a set of ivory jackstraws. We have a cat at home whose name is Rumpelstiltzken. He is very sleepy, and sleeps all day. He always picks out the most comfortable chair, and then feels very much injured if we turn him out. I like Bolivar Wiggins's story in your last paper very much. Are you going to have any more stories by Bolivar Wiggins?

"Your little friend, "HELEN CHECKERBY, aged seven.

"[We hope soon to have a new story from Mr. Wiggins, Helen. We wish we could see your cat. He seems a very sensible cat.—EDITOR *Nursery Days*.]"

## II.

"CANADA.

I am a little girl nearly ten years old, and as I like your paper very much I thought you would like a letter from me. Here is a cow's head I drew. It is not very good, but I wanted to see if I would get a prize or not. I have two little sisters; their names are Jennie and Fanny. I hope I will see my letter in print. The stories I like best are Bolivar Wiggins's story about 'Solemn Sophy' and his other one about 'Bertie's Balloon.' Have you any more stories by him? I must close now, so good-bye.

"LILLIAN JAMES.

"[Several, Lillian. Your cow is beautiful, and perhaps some day it will appear in this

column. Watch carefully, and maybe you will
see it.—EDITOR *Nursery Days*.]"

"Ah!" said Partington, softly, as he read these effusions. "That is why Bolivar Wiggins is permitted to cover so much space, eh? The children like his stories well enough to write letters about him—or perhaps Bolivar himself —ah!"

The second "ah" uttered by Partington indicated that a thought had flashed across his mind—a thought not particularly complimentary to Bolivar Wiggins.

"Perhaps," he said, slowly, "Bolivar writes these letters to the editor himself—and if Bolivar, why not I?"

It was a tempting—alas, too tempting—opportunity to supply the editor of *Nursery Days* with the needed evidence that stories of the "Tommy and the Huckleberry-tree" order were the most popular literary novelty of the day, and to it, in a moment of weakness, Partington succumbed. I regret to have to record the fact that he passed the balance of the night writing letters from fictitious "Sallies, aged six," "Warry and Georgie, twins, aged twelve," and others dwelling in widely separated sections of the country, to the number of at least two dozen, all of which, being an expert penman, Partington wrote in a diversity of juvenile hands that was worthy of a better cause. Here are two samples of the letters he wrote that night:

## I.

"NORWICH, CONNECTICUT.

"I have taken the *Nursery Days* for one year, and think it is a very nice paper. For pets I have two cats, named Lady Tompkins and Jimpsey. I have tried to solve the 'Caramel Puzzle,' but think one answer is wrong. I go to school, and there are forty-four scholars in my room. My little kitty Jimpsey sleeps all day long, and at night she is playful. She wakes me up in the morning, and then waits till I get up. Who is Mr. Smithers who wrote that beautiful story about 'Tommy and the Huckleberry-tree'? Everybody of all ages, from baby to my grandmother, likes it and hopes you will print more by that author.

"SARAH WINKLETOP."

## II.

"YONKERS, N.Y.

"Our Uncle Willie in New York sends us *Nursery Days* every week. We like it immensely, and every one tries to get the first reading of it. "Tommy and the Huckleberry-tree" is a splendid story. Papa bought six copies of *Nursery Days* with that in it to send to my little cousins in England.

"JIMMIE CONWAY RHODES."

Others were more laudatory of Partington's story, some less so, but each demanded more of his work.

These written, Partington made arrangements to have them posted from the various towns wherein they were ostensibly written, and then, when they had been posted, he chuckled slightly and sat down to await developments.

It took a trifle over one week for developments to develop, and then they developed rapidly. Just eight days after his conception of this magnificent scheme the postman whistled at Partington's door and left this note:

OFFICE OF NURSERY DAYS,

NEW YORK, *March* 16, 1889.

"*Richard Partington Smithers, Esq.*:

"DEAR SIR,—Can you call upon me some afternoon this week? Yours truly,

THOMAS JACKSONTORPYHUE,

"Editor *Nursery Days*."

"The bait is good, and I'll land the fish at once," said Partington, his face wreathing with smiles. "I'll call upon Mr. Thomas Jackson Torpyhue."

And call he did. Two hours later he entered the sanctum of the editor of *Nursery Days*.

"Good-afternoon," he said, as he sat down at the editor's side.

"Good-afternoon, Mr. Smithers," said Mr. Torpyhue. "I'm very glad to see you."

"I thought you'd be," began Partington, forgetting himself for a moment in his triumph. "If that wasn't evidence enough that I—ah– oh—er—ah! Ahem! Why, certainly," he continued, suddenly recalling the fact that as yet he could properly have no knowledge of the evidence in question.

The editor threw his head back and laughed, and Partington forced himself to join him, nervously withal.

"You have heard of the evidence have you?" asked Mr. Torpyhue.

Partington gasped faintly, and said he thought not.

"Well, it's very strange, Mr. Smithers," said Mr. Torpyhue, "but do you know that you have developed into one of our most popular authors?"

"Indeed?" queried Partington, pulling himself together and trying to appear gratified.

"Yes, sir. Here is a bundle of twenty-four letters all received within three days. One of the letters calls you the best writer of short stories of the day. Another, from Canada, written by a parent, says that you have written one of the most delightful bits of juvenile humor that he has seen in forty years."

"How extremely flattering!" said Partington, faintly.

"Yes, extremely," assented the editor, dryly. "And now, Mr. Smithers, I'm going to do for you what this paper has never done even to its most popular author in the past."

"Now, my dear Mr. Torpyhue," began Partington, gaining courage, "I beg you not to feel called upon to discriminate against your old favorites in my favor. Your present rates of payment are entirely satisfac—"

"You misunderstand me, Mr. Smithers," interrupted Mr. Torpyhue. "What I'm going to do to you that I never before have done even to our most popular author is to return to you at once every one of those highly entertaining manuscripts you have favored us with—we receive so many real letters from real children that, of course, we cannot afford to buy from you purely fictitious ones. These of yours are excellently well done, but you see my point. One does not pay for things that can be had gratis. Perhaps later you will try us with something else," he added, with a grin.

Here Mr. Torpyhue paused, and Partington tried to think of something to say. It was all so sudden, however, and, in spite of his misgivings, so extremely unexpected, that his breath was taken away. He had neither breath nor presence of mind enough left even to deny the allegation, and when he did recover his breath he found himself walking dejectedly down the stairs of the *Nursery Days* building with his bundle of encomia in his hands.

"I wonder how he caught on!" he groaned, as half an hour later he entered his room and threw himself face downward on his couch.

Investigation after dinner gave him a clue.

Not one of the letters had been mailed from the town in which it had been dated. The envelope containing the Washington letter bore the Boston postmark. The Brooklyn missive had been sent from Chicago, that from Norwich had been posted at Yonkers, and vice versa, and so on through the whole list. Each and every one had, through some evil chance, started wrong. In addition to this, Partington found that in a forgetful moment he had appended to two of the communications an editorial response promising more work from Mr. Smithers.

"I must have been muddled by my success with 'Tommy and the Huckleberry-tree,'" he sighed, as he cast the documents into the fire. "If that's the effect literary honors have on me I'd better quit the profession, which leaves only two things to be done. I shall have to commit one of two crimes—suicide or matrimony. The question now is, which?"

He thought deeply for a moment, and then, putting on his hat and overcoat, he turned off the gas and left the room.

"I'll call on Harris, borrow a cent from him, and let the toss decide," he said, as he passed out into the night.

Is it really any wonder that Mr. Smithers has given up literature?

# THE BASE INGRATITUDE OF BARKIS, M.D.

The time has arrived when it is possibly proper that I should make a note of the base ingratitude of Barkis, M.D. I have hesitated to do this hitherto for several reasons, any one of which would prove a valid excuse for my not doing so. To begin with, I have known Barkis ever since he was a baby. I have tossed him in the air, to his own delight and to the consternation of his mother, who feared lest I should fail to catch him on his way down, or that I should underestimate the distance between the top of his head and the ceiling on his way up. Later I have held him on my knee and told him stories of an elevating nature—mostly of my own composition—and have afterwards put these down upon paper and sold them to syndicates at great profit. So that, in a sense, I am beholden to Barkis for some measure of my prosperity. Then, when Barkis grew older, I taught him the most approved methods of burning his fingers on the Fourth of July, and when he went to college I am convinced that he gained material aid from me in that I loaned him my college scrap-books, which contained, among other things, a large number of examination papers which I marvel greatly to-day that I was ever able successfully to pass, and which gave to him some hint as to the ordeal he was about to go through. In his younger professional days, also, I have been Barkis's friend, and have called him up, to minister to a pain I never had, at four o'clock in the morning, simply because I had reason to believe that he needed four or five dollars to carry him through the ensuing hours of the day.

Quotation books have told us that in love, as well as in war, all is fair, and if this be true Barkis's ingratitude, the narration of which cannot now give pain to any one, becomes, after all, nothing more than a venial offence. I do not place much reliance upon the ethics of quotation books generally, but when I remember my own young days, and the things I did to discredit the other fellow in that little affair which has brought so much happiness into my own life, I am inclined to nail my flag to the masthead in defence of the principle that lovers can do no wrong. It is no ordinary stake that a lover plays for, and if he stacks the cards, and in other ways turns his back upon the guiding principles of his life, blameworthy as he may be, I shall not blame him, but shall incline rather towards applause.

On the other hand, something is due to the young ladies in the case, and as much for their sake as for any other reason have I set upon paper this narrative of the man's ingratitude, simply telling the story and drawing no conclusions whatever.

Barkis was not endowed with much in the way of worldly possessions. His father had died when the lad was very young, and had left the boy and his mother to struggle on alone. But there was that in both of them which enabled the mother to feel that the boy was worth struggling for, and the boy at a very early age to realize the difficulties of the struggle, and to like the difficulties because they afforded him an opportunity to help his mother either by not giving her unnecessary trouble or in bringing to her efforts in their mutual behalf aid of a very positive kind.

Boys of this kind—and in saying this I cast no reflections whatsoever upon that edifying race of living creatures whom I admire and respect more than any other—are so rare that it did not take the neighbors of the Barkis family many days to discover that the little chap was worth watching, and if need be caring for in a way which should prove substantial. There are so many ways, too, in which one may help a boy without impairing his self-reliance that on the whole it was not very difficult to assist Barkis. So when one of his neighbors employed him in his office at a salary of eight dollars a week, when other boys received only four for similar service, the lad, instead of feeling himself favored, assumed an obligation and made himself worth five times as much as the other boys, so that really his employer, and not he, belonged to the debtor class.

Some said it was a pity that little Barkis wasted his talents in a real estate office, but they were the people who didn't know him. He expended his nervous energy in the real estate office, but his mind he managed to keep free for the night school, and when it came to the ultimate it was found that little Barkis had wasted nothing. He entered college when several other boys—who had not served in a real estate office, who had received diplomas from the high-school, and who had played while he had studied—failed.

That his college days were a trial to his mother every one knew. She wished him to keep his end up, and he did—and without spending all that his mother sent him, either. The great trouble was that at the end of his college course it was understood that Barkis intended studying medicine. When that crept out the neighbors sighed. They deprecated the resolve among themselves, but applauded the boy's intention to his face.

"Good for you, Jack!" said one. "You are just the man for a doctor, and I'll give you all my business."

This man, of course, was a humorist.

Another said: "Jack, you are perfectly right. Real estate and coal are not for you. Go in for medicine; when my leg is cut off you shall do the cutting."

To avoid details, however, some of which would make a story in themselves, Jack Barkis went through college, studied medicine, received his diploma as a full-fledged M.D., and settled down at Dumfries Corners for practice. And practice did not come! And income was not.

It was plainly visible to the community that Barkis was hard up, as the saying is, and daily growing more so. To make matters worse, it was now impossible to help him as the boy had been helped. He was no longer a child, but a man; and the pleasing little subterfuges, which we had employed to induce the boy to think he was making his way on his own sturdy little legs, with the man were out of the question. His clothing grew threadbare, and there were stories of insufficient nourishment. As time went on the outward and visible signs of his poverty increased, yet no one could devise any plan to help him.

And then came a solution, and inasmuch as it was brought about by the S.F.M.E., an association of a dozen charming young women in the city forming the Society for Mutual Encouragement, or Enjoyment, or Endorsement, or something else beginning with E—I never could ascertain definitely what the E stood for—it would seem as if the young ladies should have received greater consideration than they did when prosperity knocked at the Doctor's door.

It seems that the Doctor attended a dance one evening in a dress coat, the quality and lack of quantity of which were a flagrant indication of a sparse, not to say extremely needy, wardrobe. All his charm of manner, his grace in the dance, his popularity, could not blind others to the fact that he was ill-dressed, and the girls decided that something must be done, and at once.

"We might give a lawn fete for his benefit," one of them suggested.

"He isn't a church or a Sunday-school," Miss Daisy Peters retorted. "Besides, I know Jack Barkis well enough to know that he would never accept charity from any one. We've got to help him professionally."

"We might boycott all the fellows at dances," suggested Miss Wilbur, "unless they will patronize the Doctor. Decline to dance with them unless they present a certificate from Jack proving that they are his patients."

"Humph!" said Miss Peters. "That wouldn't do any good. They are all healthy, and even if they did go to Jack for a prescription the chances are they wouldn't pay him. They haven't much more money than he has."

"I am afraid that is true," assented Miss Wilbur. "Indeed, if they have any at all, I can't say that they have given much sign of it this winter. The Bachelors' Cotillon fell through for lack of interest, they said, but I have my doubts on that score. It's my private opinion they weren't willing or able to pay for it."

"Well, I'm sure I don't know what we can do to help Jack. If he had our combined pocket-money he'd still be poor," sighed Miss Peters.

"He couldn't be induced to take it unless he earned it," said little Betsy Barbett. "You all know that."

"Hurrah!" cried Miss Peters, clapping her hands ecstatically; "I have it! I have it! I have it! We'll put him in the way of earning it."

And they all put their heads together, and the following was the result:

The next day Jack Barkis's telephone rang more often in an hour than it had ever done before in a month, and every ring meant a call.

The first call was from Miss Daisy Peters, and he responded.

"I'm so sorry to send for you—er—Doctor," she said—she had always called him Jack before, but now he had come professionally—"for—for—Rover, but the poor dog is awfully sick to-day, and Doctor Pruyn was out of town. Do you mind?"

"Certainly not, Daisy," he replied, a shade of disappointment on his face. I am inclined to believe he had hoped to find old Mr. Peters at death's door. "If the dog is sick I can help him. What are his symptoms?"

And Miss Peters went on to say that her cherished Rover, she thought, had malaria. He was tired and lazy, when usually he rivalled the cow that jumped over the moon in activity. She neglected to say that she had with her own fair hands given the poor beast a dose of sulphonal the night before—not enough to hurt him, but sufficient to make him appear tired and sleepy.

"I must see my patient," said the Doctor, cheerfully. "Will he come if I whistle?"

Miss Peters was disinclined to accede to this demand. She was beginning to grow fearful that Jack would see through her little subterfuge, and that the efforts of the S.F.M.E. would prove fruitless.

"Oh," she demurred, "is that—er—necessary? Rover isn't a child, you know. He won't stick out his tongue if you tell him to—and, er—I don't think you could tell much from his pulse—and—"

"I'd better see him, though," observed Jack, quietly. "I certainly can't prescribe unless I do."

So Rover was brought out, and it was indeed true that his old-time activity had been superseded by a lethargy which made the wagging of his tail a positive effort. Still, Doctor Barkis was equal to the occasion, prescribed for the dog, and on his books that night wrote down a modest item as against Mr. Billington Peters and to his own financial credit. Furthermore, he had promised to call again the next day, which meant more practice.

On his return home he found a hurry call awaiting him. Miss Betsy Barbett had dislocated her wrist. So to the Barbett mansion sped Doctor Barkis, and there, sure enough, was Miss Barbett apparently suffering greatly.

"Oh, I am so glad you have come," she moaned. "It hurts dreadfully, Jack —I mean Doctor."

"I'll fix that in a second," said he, and he did, although he thought it odd that there were no signs of any inflammation. He was not aware that one of the most cherished and fascinating accomplishments of Miss Barbett during her childhood had been her ability to throw her wrist out of joint. She could throw any of her joints out of place, but she properly chose her wrist upon this occasion as being the better joint to intrust to a young physician. If Jack had known that until his coming her wrist had been all right, and that it had not become disjointed until he rang the front door bell of the Barbett house, he might not have been so pleased as he entered the item against Judge Barbett in his book, nor would he have wondered at the lack of inflammation.

So it went. The Hicks's cook was suddenly taken ill—Mollie Hicks gave her a dollar to do it—and Jack was summoned. The Tarletons' coachman was kept out on a wet night for two hours by Janette Tarleton, and very properly contracted a cold, for which the young woman made herself responsible, and Doctor Barkis was called in. Then the society itself discovered many a case among the worthy poor needing immediate medical treatment from Barkis, M.D., and, although Jack wished to make no charge, insisted that he should, and threatened to employ some one else if he didn't.

By degrees a practice resulted from this conspiracy of the S.F.M.E., and then a municipal election came along, and each candidate for the Mayoralty was given quietly to understand by parties representing the S.F.M.E., that unless Jack Barkis was made health officer of the city he'd better look out for himself, and while both candidates vowed they had made no pledges, each had sworn ten days before election-day by all that was holy that Barkis should have this eighteen-hundred-dollar office—and he got it! Young women may not vote, but they have influence in small cities.

At the end of the second year of the S.F.M.E.'s resolve that Barkis must be cared for he was in receipt of nearly twenty-eight hundred dollars a year, could afford a gig, and so command a practice; and having obtained his start, his own abilities took care of the rest.

And then what did Jack Barkis, M.D., do? When luxuries began to manifest

29

themselves in his home—indeed, when he found himself able to rent a better one—whom did he ask to share its joys with him?

Miss Daisy Peters, who had dosed her dog that he might profit? No, indeed!

Miss Betsy Barbett, who disfigured her fair wrist in his behalf? Alas, no!

Miss Hicks, who had spent a dollar to bribe a cook that he might earn two? No, the ungrateful wretch!

Any member of the S.F.M.E.? I regret to say not.

He went and married a girl from Los Angeles, whom he met on one of the summer vacations the S.F.M.E. had put within his reach—a girl from whom no portion of his measure of prosperity had come.

Such was the ingratitude of Barkis. They have never told me so, but I think the S.F.M.E. feel it keenly. Barkis I believe to be unconscious of it—but then he is in love with Mrs. Barkis, which is proper; and as I have already indicated, when a man is in love there are a great many things he does not see —in fact, there is only one thing he does see, and that is Her Majesty, the Queen. I can't blame Barkis, and even though I was aware of the conspiracy to make him prosperous, I did not think of the ungrateful phase of it all until I spoke to Miss Peters about his *fiancée*, who had visited Dumfries Corners.

"She's charming," said I. "Don't you think so?"

"Oh yes," said Miss Peters, dubiously.

"But I don't see why Jack went to Los Angeles for a wife."

"Ah?" said I. "Maybe it was the only place where he could find one."

"Thank you!" snapped Miss Peters. "For my part, I think the Dumfries Corners girls are quite as attractive—ah—Betsy Barbett for instance—or any other girl in Jack's circle."

"Like yourself?" I smiled.

"My!" she cried. "How can you say such a thing?"

And really I was sorry I had said it. It seemed so like twitting a person on facts, when I came to think about it.

# THE UTILITARIAN MR. CARRAWAY

The Christmas season was approaching, and Mr. Carraway, who had lately become something of a philosopher, began to think about gifts for his wife and children. The more he thought of them, the more firmly was he convinced that there was something radically wrong with the system of giving that had prevailed in past years. He conjured up visions of the useless things he had given and received on previous occasions, and an inventory of his personal receipts at the four celebrations leading up to the present disclosed the fact that he was long on match-boxes, cigar-cases, and smoking-jackets, the last every one of them too small, with an appalling supply of knitted and crocheted objects, the gifts of his children, in reserve. His boot-closet was a perfect revelation of the misdirected Christmas energies of the young, disclosing, as it always did upon occasions when he was in a great hurry, a half-dozen pairs of worsted slippers, which he had received at Yuletide, some of them adorned with stags of beads leaping over zephyr walls, and others made in the image of cats of extraordinary color, with yellow glass eyes set in directly over the toe whereon he kept his favorite corn. I am not sure that it was not the stepping of an awkward visitor upon one of these same glass eyes, while these slippers for the first time covered his feet, that set Mr. Carraway to cogitating upon the hollowness of "Christmas as She is Celebrated." Indeed, it is my impression that at the very moment when that bit of adornment was pressed down upon Mr. Carraway's corn he announced rather forcibly his disbelief in the utility of any such infernal Christmas present as that. And as time went on, and that offending, staring slipper slipped into his hand every time he searched the closet in the dark for a left patent-leather pump, or some other missing bit of foot-gear, the conviction grew upon him that of the great reforms of which the world stood in crying need, the reformation of the Christmas gift was possibly the most important.

The idea grew to be a mania with him, and he gradually developed into a utilitarian of the most pronounced type. Nothing in the world so suited him as an object, homely or otherwise, that could be used for something; the things that were used for nothing had no attractions for him. After this he developed further, and discovered new uses for old objects. Mrs. Carraway's parlor vases were turned into receptacles for matches, or papers, according to their size. The huge Satsuma vase became a more or less satisfactory bill-file; and the cloisonné jar, by virtue of its great durability, Mr. Carraway used as a receptacle for the family golf-balls, much to the trepidation of his good wife, who considered that the vase, like some women, had in its beauty a sufficient cause for existence, and who would have preferred going without golf forever to the destruction of her treasured bit of bric-à-brac.

Mrs. Carraway did her best to stay the steady advance in utilitarianism of her husband. She could bide with him in most matters. In fact, until it came to the use of the cloisonné jar for a golf-ball reservoir, she considered the idea at least harmless, and was forced to admit that it indeed held many good points.

"I think it is perfectly proper," she said, "to consider all things from the point of view of their utility. I do not believe in sending a ball-dress to a poor woman who is starving or suffering for want of coal, but I must say, John, that you carry your theory too far when you insist on using an object for some purpose for which it was manifestly never intended."

"But who is to say what a thing is manifestly made for?" demanded Carraway. "You don't know, or at least you can't say positively, what one of many possible uses the designer and maker of any object had in mind when he designed and made that especial object. This particular vase was fashioned by a heathen. It is beautiful and graceful, but beyond producing something beautiful and graceful, how can you say what other notion that heathen had as to its possible usefulness? He may have made it to hold flowers. He may have intended it for a water-jug. He may have considered it a suitable receptacle in which its future favored owner might keep his tobacco, or his opium, or any one of the thousand and one things that you can put in a vase with a hope of getting it out again."

"Well, we know he didn't intend it for golf-balls, anyhow," said Mrs. Carraway. "For the very simple reason that the heathen don't play golf."

"They may play some kind of a game which is a heathen variation of golf," observed Mr. Carraway, coldly.

"That couldn't be," persisted Mrs. Carraway. "judging from the effect of Sunday golf-playing on church attendance, I don't think anything more completely pagan than golf could be found. However—"

"But the fact remains, my dear," Carraway interrupted, "that while we may surmise properly enough that the original maker of an object did not intend it to be used for certain purposes, you cannot say positively, because you don't know that your surmise is absolutely correct."

"But I think you can," said Mrs. Carraway. "In fact, *I* will say positively that the man who made our new frying-pan made it to fry things in, and not to be used in connection with a tack-hammer as a dinner-gong. I know that the hardware people who manufactured our clothes-boiler, down in the laundry, did not design it as a toy bass-drum for the children to bang on on the morning of the Fourth of July. I would make a solemn affidavit to the fact that the maker of a baby-carriage never dreamed of its possible use as an impromptu toboggan for a couple of small boys to coast downhill on in midsummer. Yet these things have been used for these various purposes in our own household experience. A megaphone can be used as a beehive, and a hammock can be turned into a fly-net for a horse, but you never think of doing so; and, furthermore, you *can* say positively that while the things may be used for these purposes, the original maker never, never, never thought of it."

"Nonsense," said Carraway, wilting a little. "Nonsense. You argue just like a woman—"

"I think that was what I was designed for," laughed Mrs. Carraway. "Of course I do."

"Oh! but what I mean is that you take utterly ridiculous and extreme cases. The things never could happen. Who'd ever dream of making a beehive out of a megaphone?"

"Oh, I think it might occur to the same ingenious mind that discovered that a cloisonné vase would hold golf-balls," smiled Mrs. Carraway.

Carraway laughed. "There you go again," he said. "I wonder why women can't argue without becoming ridiculous? It would be mighty poor economy to pay $4 for a megaphone as a substitute for a $2 beehive."

"That is true," said Mrs. Carraway. "I never thought of that."

"Of course you didn't," retorted Carraway, triumphantly. "Of course you didn't; and that's what I mean when I say you argue like a woman. You get hold of what seems on the surface to be a regular solar-plexus retort, and fail to see how it becomes a boomerang before you can say Jack Robinson."

"I suppose if I hadn't been worried about the vase I would have thought of it," said Mrs. Carraway, meekly. "It worries me to see a $150 vase used for a purpose that a fifty-cent calico bag would serve quite as well."

Carraway glanced searchingly at his wife.

"Well—ah—hem!" he said. "Quite right, my dear, quite right. I think, on the whole, you would better get the calico bag."

For a few days after this little discussion Carraway was very reticent about his utilitarian ideas. The more he thought of his wife's retort the less secure he felt in his own position, and he was very sorry he had spoken about boomerangs and solar-plexus retorts. But with time he recovered his equanimity, and early in December returned to his old ways.

"I've just been up in the attic," he said to his wife one Sunday afternoon, when he appeared on the scene rather dusty of aspect. "There's a whole lot of useful stuff up there going to waste. I found four old beaver hats, any one of which would make a very good waste-basket for the spare bedroom if it was suitably trimmed; and I don't see why you don't take these straw hats of mine and make work-baskets of them."

Here he held out two relics of bygone fashions to his wife. Mrs. Carraway took them silently. She was so filled with suppressed laughter over her husband's suggestions that she hardly dared to speak lest she should give way to her mirth, and a man does not generally appreciate mirth at his own expense after he has been rummaging in an attic for an hour or more, filling his lungs and covering his clothes and hands with dust.

However, after a moment she managed to blurt out, "Perhaps I can make one of them dainty enough to send to your mother for her Christmas present."

"I was about to suggest that very same thing," said Carraway, brushing the dust from his sleeve. "Either you could send it or Mollie"—Mollie was Mr. Carraway's small daughter. "I think Mollie's grandmother would be more pleased with a gift of that kind than with one of the useless little fallals that children give their grandparents on Christmas Day. What did she give her last year?"

The question was opportune, for it gave Mrs. Carraway a chance to laugh outright with some other ostensible object than her husband. She availed herself of the chance, threw her head back, and shook convulsively.

"She sent her a ball of shaving-paper," Mrs. Carraway said.

A faint smile flitted over Carraway's face. "Well, it might have been worse," he said. "She can use it for curling-paper." He paused a moment. Then he said: "I want to say to you, my dear, that—ah—I want Christmas celebrated this year after my plan of selection. Instead of squandering our hard-earned dollars on things no sensible person wants and none can use, we will consider, first of all, practical utility."

"Very well," sighed Mrs. Carraway. "I quite agree as far as you and I are concerned—but how about the children? I don't think Tommie would feel very happy to wake up on Christmas morning and find a pair of suspenders and a new suit of clothes under the tree. He needs both, but he wants tin soldiers. And as for Mollie, she expects a doll."

"Well, I don't wish to be hard on the children," said Mr. Carraway, "but now is the time to begin training them. There may be a temporary disappointment, but in the end they will be happier for it. Of course I don't say to give them necessities of life for Christmas, but in selecting what we do give them, get something useful. Dolls and tin soldiers and toy balloons are well enough in their way, but they are absolutely useless. Therefore, I say, don't give them such things. Surely Mollie would be pleased to receive a nice little fur tippet or a muff, and I'll get Tommie a handsome snow-shovel, that he can use when he cleans off the paths. He won't mind; it will be a gift worth having, and by degrees he'll come to see that the plan of utility is a good one."

Mrs. Carraway discreetly held her tongue, although she was far from approving Carraway's course in so far as it affected the children. She tacitly agreed to the proposition, but there was the light of an idea in her eye.

The days intervening before Christmas passed rapidly away, and Christmas eve finally came. Tommie and Mollie were bubbling over with suppressed excitement, and frequently went off into spasms of giggles. There was something very funny in the wind evidently. After dinner the small family repaired to the library, where the children were in the habit of distributing their gifts for their parents on the night before Christmas. Mrs. Carraway was beaming, and so was Mr. Carraway. The children had been informed of what they were to expect, and after an hour or two of regret, they had put their little heads together, giggled a half-dozen times, and accepted the situation.

"Your mother has presented me with a ton of coal, children," said Carraway, smiling happily. "Now you may think that a funny sort of gift—"

"Yeth, papa," said Mollie.

"Awful funny," said Tommie, wiggling with glee.

"Well, it does seem so at first, but, now, how much better to give me that than to present me with something that I could look at for a few days and then would have no further use for!"

"That's so, pa," said Mollie.

"I guess you're right," said Tommie. "Wat cher got for ma?"

"I have given her a brand-new set of china for the dining-room," said Mr. Carraway.

"And it was just what I needed," said Mrs. Carraway, happily. "And now, children, go up-stairs, and bring down your presents for your father."

The children sped noisily out of the room and up the stairs.

"I hope you impressed it on their minds that I wanted nothing useless?" said Carraway.

"I did," said Mrs. Carraway. "I explained the whole thing to them, and told them what they might expect to receive. Then I gave them each ten dollars of the money they'd saved, and let them go shopping on their own account. I don't know what they bought you, but it's something huge."

Mrs. Carraway had hardly finished when the two giggling tots came into the room, carrying with difficulty a parcel, which, as Mrs. Carraway had said, was indeed huge. Mr. Carraway eyed it with curiosity as the string was unfastened and the package burst open.

"There," cried Tommie, breathlessly.

"It's all for you, pa, from Mollie and me."

The two children stood to one side. Mrs. Carraway appeared surprised in an amused fashion, while Carraway stood appalled at what lay before him, as well he might; for the package contained a great wax doll with deep staring blue eyes, a small doll's house with two floors in it and a front door that opened, china and chairs and table and bureaus in miniature to furnish the house—indeed, all the paraphernalia of a well-ordered residence for a French doll. Besides these were two boxes of tin soldiers, cannon, tents, swords, a fully equipped lead army, a mechanical fish, and a small zinc steamboat, suitable for a cruise in a bath-tub.

Carraway looked at the children, and the children looked at Carraway.

"Why," said he, as soon as he could recover his equanimity, "there must be some mistake."

"No," said Mollie. "We picked 'em out for you ourselves. We thought you'd need 'em."

Mrs. Carraway turned away to cough slightly.

"Need them?" demanded Carraway with a perplexed frown. "When?"

"Oh—to-morrow," said Tommie.

"What for?" demanded Carraway.

"*Why, to give to us, of course*" said the children in chorus.

---

"My dear," said Carraway, two hours later, after the children had retired, "I've been thinking this thing over."

"Yes?" said Mrs. Carraway.

"Yes," said Carraway; "and I've made up my mind that those children of ours are born geniuses. I don't believe, after all, they could have selected anything which would be more satisfactorily useful in the present emergency."

"Well," observed Mrs. Carraway, quietly, "I don't either. I thought so at the time when they asked my permission to do their shopping at the International Toy Bazar."

"It's a solar-plexus retort, just the same," said Carraway, as he shook his head and went to bed. "I think on the 1st of January, if you have no objections, Mrs. Carraway, I will forswear utilitarianism—and you may remove the golf-balls from the cloisonné vase as soon as you choose."

# THE BOOK SALES OF MR. PETERS

Like many another town which frankly confesses itself to be a "city of the third class," Dumfries Corners is not only well provided but somewhat overburdened with impecunious institutions of a public and semi-public nature. The large generosity of persons who never give to, but are often identified with, churches, hospitals, associations of philanthropic intent of one kind and another, in Dumfries Corners as elsewhere, is frequently the cause of embarrassment to persons who do give without being lavish of the so-called influence of their names. There are quite a dozen individuals out of the forty thousand souls who live in that favored town who find it convenient to give away as much as five hundred dollars annually for the maintenance of milk dispensaries, hospitals, and other deserving enterprises of similar nature for the needy. Yet at the close of each fiscal year those who have given to this extent are invariably confronted by "reports," issued by officials of the various institutions, frankly confessing failure to make both ends meet, and everybody wonders why more interest has not been taken. "Surely, we have loaned our names!" they say. It never occurs to anybody that one successful charity is better than six failures. It has never entered into the minds of the managers of these enterprises that a man disposed to give away five hundred dollars could make his contributions to the public welfare more efficacious by giving the whole to one institution instead of dividing it among twenty.

However, human nature is the same everywhere, and until the crack of doom sounds mankind will be found undertaking more charity than it can carry through successfully, not only in Dumfries Corners, but everywhere else. It would be difficult to fix the responsibility for this state of affairs, although the large generosity of those who lend their names and blockade their pockets may consider itself a candidate for chief honors in this somewhat vital matter. It may be, too, that the large generosity of people who really are largely generous with their thousands has something to do with it. There is more than one ten-thousand-dollar town in existence which has accepted a hundred-thousand-dollar hospital from generously disposed citizens, and the other citizens thereof have properly hailed their benefactor's name with loud acclaim, but the hundred-thousand-dollar hospital, which might have been a fifty-thousand-dollar hospital, with an endowment of fifty thousand more to make it self-supporting, has a tendency to ruin other charities quite as worthy, because its maintenance pumps dry the pockets of those who have to give. It will require a drastic course of training, I fear, to open the eyes of the public to the fact that even generosity can be overdone, and I must disclaim any desire to superintend the process of securing their awakening, for it is an ungrateful task to criticise even a mistakenly generous person; and man being by nature prone to thoughtless judgments, the critic of a philanthropist who spends a million of dollars to provide tortoise-shell combs for bald beggars would shortly find himself in hot water. Therefore let us discuss not the causes, but some of the results of the system which has placed upon suburban shoulders such seemingly hopeless philanthropic burdens. At Dumfries Corners the book sales of Mr. Peters, one of the vestrymen, were one of these results.

There were two of these sales. The first, like all book sales for charity, consisted largely of the vending of ice-cream and cake. The second was different; but I shall not deal with that until I have described the first.

This had been given at Mr. Peters's house, with the cheerful consent of Mrs. Peters. The object was to raise seventy-five dollars, the sum needed to repair the roof of Mr. Peters's church. In ordinary times the congregation could have advanced the seventy-five dollars necessary to keep the rain from trickling through the roof and leaking in a steady stream upon the pew of Mrs. Bumpkin, a lady too useful in knitting sweaters for the heathen in South Africa to be ignored. But in that year of grace,

1897, there had been so many demands made upon everybody, from the Saint William's Hospital for Trolley Victims, from the Mistletoe Inn, a club for workingmen which was in its initial stages and most worthily appealed to the public purse, and for the University Extension Society, whose ten-cent lectures were attended by the swellest people in Dumfries Corners and their daughters—and so on—that the collections of Saint George's had necessarily fallen off to such an extent that plumbers' bills were almost as much of a burden to the rector as the needs of missionaries in Borneo for dress-suits and golf-clubs. In this emergency, Mr. Peters, whose account at his bank had been overdrawn by his check which had paid for painting the Sunday-school room pink in order that the young religious idea might be taught to shoot under more roseate circumstances than the blue walls would permit, and so could not well offer to have the roof repaired at his own expense, suggested a book sale.

"We can get a lot of books on sale from publishers," he said, "and I haven't any doubt that Mrs. Peters will be glad to have the affair at our house. We can surely raise seventy-five dollars in this way. Besides, it will draw the ladies in the congregation together."

The offer was accepted. Mrs. Peters acquiesced. Peters and his co-workers asked favors and got them from friends in the publishing world. The day came. The books arrived, and the net results to the Roofing Fund of Saint George's were gratifying. The vestry had asked for seventy-five dollars, and the sale actually cleared eighty-three! To be sure, Mr. Wiggins spent fifty dollars at the sale. And Mrs. Thompson spent forty-nine. And the cake-table took in thirty-eight. And the ice-cream was sold, thanks to the voracity of the children, for nineteen dollars. And some pictures which had been donated by Mrs. Bumpkin sold for thirty-one dollars, and the gambling cakes, with rings and gold dollars in them, cleared fifteen. Still, when it was all reckoned up, eighty-three dollars stood to the credit of the roof! In affairs of this kind, results, not expenses, are considered.

Surely the venture was a success. Although from the point of view of bringing the ladies of the congregation together—well, the less said about that the better. In any event, parts of Dumfries Corners were cooler the following summer than they had ever been before.

And then, in the natural sequence of events, the next year came. The hospital, and the inn, and the various other institutions of the city indorsed by prominent names, but void of resources, as usual, left the church so poor that something had to be done to repair the cellar of Saint George's by outside effort, water leaking in from the street. The matter was discussed, and the amount needed was settled upon. This time Saint George's needed ninety dollars. It didn't really need so much, but it was thought well to ask for more than was needed, "because then, you know, you're more likely to get it."

The book-cake-and-cream sale of the year before had been so successful that everybody said: "By all means let us have another literary afternoon at Mr. Peters's."

"All right!" said Peters, calmly, when the project was suggested. "Certainly! Of course! Have anything you please at my house. Not that I am running a casino, but that I really enjoy turning my house inside out in a good cause once in a while," he added, with a smile which those about him believed to be sincere. "Only," said he, "kindly make me master of ceremonies on this occasion."

"Certainly!" replied the vestry. "If this thing is to be in your house you ought to have everything to say about it."

"I ask for control," said Peters, "not because I am fond of power, but because experience has taught me that somebody should control affairs of this sort."

"Certainly," was the reply again, and Peters was made a committee of one, with power to run the sale in his own way, and the vestry settled down in that calm and contented frame of mind which goes with the consciousness of solvency.

Three months elapsed, and nothing was done. No cards were issued from the home of Peters announcing a sale of any kind, cake, cream, or books, and the literary afternoon seemed to have sunk into oblivion. The chairman of the Committee on Supplies, however, having gone into the cellar one morning to inspect the coal reserve, found himself obliged either to wade knee deep in water or to neglect his duty—and, of course, being a sensible man, he chose the latter course. He knew that in impecunious churches willing candidates for vestry honors were rare, and he, therefore, properly saved himself for future use. Wading in water might have brought on pneumonia, and he was aware that there really isn't any reason why a man should die for a cause if there is a reasonable excuse for his living in the same behalf. But he went home angry.

"That cellar isn't repaired yet," he said to his wife. "You'd think from the quantity of water there that ours was a Baptist church instead of the Church of England."

"It's a shame!" ejaculated his wife, who, having that morning finished embroidering a centre-piece for the dinner-table of the missionaries in Madagascar, was full of conscious rectitude. "A perfect shame; who's to blame, dear?"

"Peters," replied the chairman. "Same old story. He makes all sorts of promises, and never carries 'em out. He thinks that just because he pays a few bills we haven't anything to say. But he'll find out his mistake. I'll call him down. I'll write him a letter he won't forget in a hurry. If he wasn't willing to attend to the matter he had no business to accept the responsibility. I'll write and tell him so."

And then, the righteous wrath of the chairman of the Committee on Supplies having expended itself in this explosion at his own dinner-table, that good gentleman forgot all about it, did not write the letter, and in fact never thought of the matter again until the next meeting of the vestry, when he suavely and jokingly inquired if the Committee on Leaks and Book Sales had any report to make. To his surprise Mr. Peters responded at once.

"Yes, gentlemen," he said, taking a check out of his pocket and handing it to the treasurer. "The Committee on Leaks, Literature, and Lemonade reports that the leak is still in excellent condition and is progressing daily, while the Literature and Lemonade have produced the very gratifying sum of one hundred and thirty-seven dollars and sixty-three cents, a check for which I have just handed the treasurer."

Even the rector looked surprised.

"Pretty good result, eh?" said Peters. "You ask for ninety dollars and get one hundred and thirty-seven dollars and sixty-three cents. You can spend a hundred dollars now on the leak and make a perfect leak of it, and have a balance of thirty-seven dollars and sixty-three cents to buy books for the Hottentots or to invest in picture-books for the Blind Asylum library."

"Ah—Mr. Peters," said the chairman of the Committee on Supplies, "I—ah —I was not aware that you'd had the sale. I—ah—I didn't receive any notice."

"Oh yes—we had it," said Peters, rubbing his hands together buoyantly. "We had it last night, and it went off superbly."

"I am sorry," said the chairman of the Committee on Supplies. "I should like to have been there."

"I didn't know of it myself, Mr. Peters," said the rector, "but I am glad it was so successful. Were there many present?"

"Well—no," said Peters. "Not many. Fact is, Mrs. Peters and the treasurer here and I were the only persons present, gentlemen. But the results sought were more than accomplished."

"I don't see exactly how, unless we are to regard this check as a gift," observed the chairman of the Committee on Supplies, coldly.

"Well, I'll tell you how," said Peters. "The check isn't a gift at all. Last year you had a book sale at my house, and this year you voted to have another. I couldn't very well object—didn't want to, in fact. Very glad to have it as long as I was allowed to control it. But last year we cleared up a bare eighty dollars. This year we have cleared up one hundred and thirty-seven dollars and sixty-three cents. Last year's book sale cost me one hundred and twenty-five dollars. The children who attended, aided and abetted by my own, spilled so much ice cream on my dining-room rug that Mrs. Peters was forced to send it to the cleaners. A very charming young woman whose name I shall not mention placed a chocolate eclair upon my library sofa while she inspected a volume of Gibson's drawings. Another equally charming young woman sat down upon it, and, whatever it did to her dress, that eclair effectually ruined the covering of my sofa. Then, as you may remember, the sale of books took place in my library, and I had the pleasure of seeing, too late, one of our sweetest little saleswomen replenishing her stock from my shelves. She had sold out all the books that had been provided, and in a mad moment of enthusiasm for the cause parted with a volume I had secured after much difficulty in London to complete a set of some rarity for about seven dollars less than the book had cost."

"Why did you not object?" demanded the chairman of the Committee on Supplies.

"My dear sir," said Mr. Peters, "I never object to anything my guests may do, particularly if they are charming and enthusiastic young women engaged in church work. But I learned a lesson, and last night's book sale was the result. If the chairman of the Committee on Supplies demands it, here is a full account of receipts."

Mr. Peters handed over a memorandum which read as follows:

Saving on Floors by not having Book Sale,     $18.00
Saving on Carpets by not having Book Sale,    6.50
Saving on Library by not having Book Sale,    29.00
Saving on Time by not having Book Sale,       50.00
Saving on Furniture by not having Book Sale   28.27
Saving on Incidentals by not having Book Sale 5.86
                              Total   $137.63

"With this statement, gentlemen," said Mr. Peters, suavely, "should the Finance Committee require it, I am prepared to submit the vouchers which show how much wear and tear on a house is required to raise eighty dollars for the heathen."

"That," said the chairman of the Finance Committee, "will not be necessary —though—" and he added this wholly jocularly, "though I don't think Mr. Peters should have charged for his time; fifty dollars is a good deal of money."

"He didn't charge for his time," murmured the treasurer. "In this statement he has paid for it!"

"Still," said he of Supplies, "the social end of it has been wiped out."

"Of course it has," retorted Mr. Peters. "And a very good thing it has been, too. Did you ever know of a church function that did not arouse animosities among the women, Mr. Squills?"

The gentleman, in the presence of men of truth, had to admit that he never knew of such a thing.

"Then what's the matter with my book sale?" demanded Peters. "It has raised more money than last year; has cost me no more—and there won't be any social volcanoes for the vestry to sit over during the coming year."

A dead silence came over all.

"I move," said Mr. Jones, at whose house the meeting was held, "that we go into executive session. Mrs. Jones has provided some cold birds, and a—ah—salad."

Mr. Jones's motion was carried, and before the meeting finally adjourned under the genial influence of good-fellowship and pleasant converse Mr. Peters's second book sale was voted to have been of the best quality.

# THE VALOR OF BRINLEY

However differentiated from other suburban places Dumfries Corners may be in most instances, in the matter of obtaining and retaining efficient domestics the citizens of that charming town find it much like all other communities of its class. Civilization brings with it everywhere, it would seem, problems difficult of solution, and conspicuous among them may be mentioned the servant problem. It is probable that the only really happy young couple that ever escaped the annoyance of this particular evil were Adam and Eve, and as one recalls their case it was the interference of a third party, in the matter of their diet, that brought all their troubles upon them, so that even they may not be said to have enjoyed complete immunity from domestic trials. What quality it is in human nature that leads a competent housemaid or a truly-talented culinary artist to abhor the country-side, and to prefer the dark, cellar-like kitchens of the city houses it is difficult to surmise; why the suburban housekeeper finds her choice limited every autumn to the maid that the city folks have chosen to reject is not clear. That these are the conditions which confront surburban residents only the exceptionally favored rustic can deny.

In Dumfries Corners, even were there no rich red upon the trees, no calendar upon the walls, no invigorating tonic in the air to indicate the season, all would know when autumn had arrived by the anxious, hunted look upon the faces of the good women of that place as they ride on the trains to and from the intelligence offices of the city looking for additions to their *ménage*. Of course in Dumfries Corners, as elsewhere, it is possible to employ home talent, but to do this requires larger means than most suburbanites possess, for the very simple reason that the home talent is always plentifully endowed with dependents. These latter, to the number of eight or ten—which observation would lead one to believe is the average of the successful local cook, for instance—increase materially the butcher's and grocer's bills, and, one not infrequently suspects, the coal man's as well.

Years ago, when he was young and inexperienced, the writer of this narrative, his suspicions having been aroused by the seeming social popularity of his cook, took occasion one Sunday afternoon to count the number of mysterious packages, of about a pound in weight each, which set forth from his kitchen and were carried along his walk in various stages of ineffectual concealment by the lady's visitors. The result was by no means appalling, seven being the total. But granting that seven was a fair estimate of the whole week's output, and that the stream flowed on Sundays only, and not steadily through the other six days, the annual output, on a basis of fifty weeks—giving the cook's generosity a two weeks' vacation—three hundred and fifty pounds of something were diverted from his pantry into channels for which they were not originally designed, and on a valuation of twenty-five cents apiece his minimum contribution to his cook's dependents became thereby very nearly one hundred dollars. Add to this the probable gifts to similarly fortunate relatives of a competent local waitress, of an equally generously disposed laundress with cousins, not to mention the genial, open-handed generosity of a hired man in the matter of kindling-wood and edibles, and living becomes expensive with local talent to help.

It is in recognition of this seemingly cast-iron rule that local service is too expensive for persons of modest income, that the modern economical house-wife prefers to fill her *ménage* with maids from the metropolis, even though it happen that she must take those who for one reason or another have failed to please her city sisters. It may be, too, that this is one of the reasons for the constant changes in most suburban houses, for it is equally axiomatic that once an alien becomes acclimated she takes on a *clientèle* of adopted relatives, who in the course of time become as much of a drain upon the treasury of the household as the Simon-Pure article.

The Brinleys had been through the domestic mill in its every phase. They had had cooks, and cooks, and cooks, and maids, and maids, and maids, plus other maids; they had been face to face with arson and murder; Mrs. Brinley had parted a laundress armed with a flat-iron from a belligerent cook armed with an ice-pick, and twice the ministers of the law had carried certain irate women bodily forth with the direst of threats lest they should return later and remove the Brinley family from the list of the living.

All of which contributed to Mrs. Brinley's unhappiness and rather increased than diminished her natural timidity. Brinley, on the other hand, professed to know no fear, but according to his theory that ways and means were his care, and that the domestic affairs of his household were his wife's, and beyond his jurisdiction, held himself aloof and said never a word to the recalcitrant servant, confining what upbraiding he did exclusively to Mrs. Brinley.

"Why don't you scold Bridget?" cried Mrs. Brinley one morning, after Brinley had made a few remarks to his wife which were not to her taste, inasmuch as she felt that she had done nothing to deserve them. "I didn't burn the steak."

"That is very true, my dear," said Brinley, "but you are responsible for the cook who did. It would never do for me to interfere. I have troubles enough with my office-boys. This is your bailiwick, not mine, and until I ask you to scold my clerks you mustn't ask me to scold your servants." With this sage remark the valiant Brinley at once took his departure.

Time passed, and it so happened one autumn that the once happy household found itself in the throes of a particularly aggravated case of cook. She was a sixteen-dollar cook, and had been recommended as being "splendid." In just what respect she showed her splendor, save in her regal lack of manners and the marvellous coloring of her costumes on her Sundays out, was never perceptible, but one thing that was wholly clear at the end of a three-weeks' service was her independence of manner.

Meals were never ready on time, and the dinner-hour, instead of being a fixed time beneath her sway, seemed to become a variable point, according to the lady's whim. In the observance of the breakfast-hour she was equally erratic, and on several trying occasions Brinley was on the verge of the dilemma of either failing to keep an appointment in town or going without his morning meal. Sometimes the coffee would come to the table a thin, amber fluid that tasted like particularly bad consommé. Again it would be served with all the thickness of a *purée*. Her bread was similarly variable in its undesirability. There were biscuits that held all the flaky charm of a snowball. There were loaves of bread that reminded one of the stories of hardtack in Cuba during the late unpleasantness. There were English muffins that rested upon poor Brinley's digestion as the world may fairly be presumed to rest upon the shoulders of Atlas, and, indeed, it is a tradition in the Brinley family that one of this cook's pie-crusts rivalled Harveyized steel in its impenetrability.

Indeed, Brinley, usually a silent sufferer, commented upon this cohesive quality of Ellen's pastry on two different occasions. On the first he advised Mrs. Brinley to learn the secret of Ellen's manipulation of the ingredients of a pie-crust, and have herself capitalized to rival the corporations which provide the government with armor-plate. On the second he made the sage though disagreeable remark that the "next apple-pie we have should be served with individual steam-drills." And he one day accompanied Mrs. Brinley to a quiet golf links, and, when he had teed up, that good lady observed one of Ellen's doughnuts upon the little mound of sand before him instead of his favorite ball.

"I cut up the Silverton ball so," he said, as he addressed the tee, "that I'm ashamed of myself. I may not play any better with this doughnut, but it will never show the marks of the irons as a bit of mere gutta-percha would."

"If you feel that way about Ellen," Mrs. Brinley observed, just as Brinley was about to drive off with a real ball, "I don't see why you don't discharge her."

Brinley took his eye off the ball to look indignantly upon his wife, and consequently foozled.

"Discharge her? Why should I discharge her?" he demanded, his temper growing as he observed where he had landed his ball. "I'm not running the house, my dear. You are. I didn't ask you to tell Miss Flossie Fairfax that, as she couldn't spell, she was no longer useful as a stenographer in the office of Brinley & Rutherford. Why should you ask me to tell a cook that her services are no longer required in the establishment of Brinley & Brinley, of which you are the manager?"

"It isn't easy to discharge a girl," Mrs. Brinley began. "Particularly a quarrelsome woman like Ellen."

"Oh, that's it," said Brinley. "You are afraid of her."

"Not exactly," said Mrs. Brinley. "But—"

"Of course, if you are afraid of her, I'll get rid of her," persisted Brinley, valiantly. "Just wait until we get home. I'll show you a thing or two when it comes to ridding one's self of an unfaithful servant. The steak this morning looked like a stake that martyrs had been burned at, and I am not afraid to say so."

And so it was decided that Brinley, on his return home, should interview Ellen and inform her that her services would not be required after the first of the month.

"Now let's play golf," he said. "I'll settle Ellen in a minute. Fore!"

How Brinley fulfilled his promise is best shown by his talk with Mrs. Brinley the next morning when, somewhat red of face, he rejoined her in the dining-room after his interview with Ellen.

"Well?" said Mrs. Brinley.

"It's all right," Brinley replied, with an uneasy glance at his wife. "She's going to stay."

"Going to stay?" echoed Mrs. Brinley, her eyes opening wide in a very natural astonishment. "Why, I thought you were going to discharge her?"

"Well—I was," he said, haltingly. "I was, of course. That's what I went down for—but—er—you know, my dear, that there are two sides to every question."

"Even to Ellen's biscuits?" Mrs. Brinley laughed.

"Never mind that. She's going to do better," said Brinley. "You'll find that hereafter we've got a cook, and not an incendiary nor a forger of armor-plate."

"And may I ask how this wonderful reform has been worked in the brief space of ten minutes?" asked Mrs. Brinley. "Have you hypnotized her?"

"No," said Brinley. Then he looked rather sheepishly out of the window. "I've given her an incentive to do better. I've increased her wages."

Mrs. Brinley gazed at him silently in open-mouthed wonder for a full half-minute.

"You did what?" asked Mrs. Brinley.

"I told her we'd give her twenty dollars a month instead of sixteen," said Brinley. "You needn't laugh," he added. "I began very severely. Asked her what she meant by ignoring our wishes as to hours. I dilated forcefully upon her apparent fondness for burning steaks to a crisp, and sending broiled chicken to the table looking as if somebody had dropped a flat-iron on them."

"Good!" exclaimed Mrs. Brinley. "And what did she say? Was she impertinent?"

"Not a bit of it," said Brinley "She took it very nicely until I spoke of the muffins, after which I had intended to give her notice to quit, but she took the wind completely out of my sails by asking me what I expected at sixteen dollars a month."

"Ah!" said Mrs. Brinley.

"Exactly," said Brinley. "That was a point I had not considered at all. After all, she was right. What can you expect for sixteen dollars?"

"Well, what next?" asked Mrs. Brinley, her eyes a-twinkle.

"I asked her if she thought she could do better on twenty dollars," he answered. "She thought she could, and that's the way it stands now."

"I see," said Mrs. Brinley, and then she burst into a perfect explosion of laughter, which she soon curbed, however, as she noticed the expression on poor Brinley's face. "I've no doubt you have acted with perfect justice in this matter, my dear George," she said. "But I think hereafter I'll do my own discharging. Your way is rather extravagant—er—don't you really think so?"

"Perhaps," said Brinley, and departed for town.

"The madam is right about that," he said to himself later in the day, as he thought over the incident. "But extravagant or not, I couldn't have discharged that woman if somebody had offered me a clear hundred. Mrs. B. doesn't know it, but I was in a blue funk from start to finish."

In which surmise Brinley was wrong. Mrs. B. did know it, and when two weeks later Ellen became absolutely impossible, and demanded a kitchen-maid as the perquisite of a twenty-dollar cook, Mrs. Brinley didn't think of calling upon her husband to perform the function of the executioner, but like a brave woman actually summoned the cook into her presence and did it herself. A less courageous woman would have gone downstairs into the kitchen to do it.

# WILKINS

It was a rather remarkable affair, taken altogether. Wilkins was not what one would call an attractive man, and none of the young women of Dumfries Corners who had met him had ever manifested anything but a pronounced aversion to his society.

"I'd rather be a wall-flower than dance with Sam Wilkins," one of these young women had said. "He not only can't dance, but, what is infinitely worse, he doesn't know that he can't dance, and as for his conversation—well, give me silence."

"You are perfectly right about that," said another. "Whenever I see him about to waltz or two-step, I immediately remove myself from the scene, and pray for the girl he's dancing with. He is a train-wrecker, and the favorite resting-place for his heels is on some one else's foot. I've heard that he steps on his own feet, too, he's so awkward, and I hope he does if it hurts him as much as he hurts me when he steps on mine."

For Wilkins's sake I am very sorry to say that this feeling towards him was invariable. I never cared much for him myself, but I felt rather sorry for him when I perceived the persistent snubbing with which he was everywhere received. He never seemed aware of it himself, happily, however, and accepted my merely sympathetic attentions with that superciliousness which always goes with conscious rectitude.

Conscious rectitude, I think, was Wilkins's trouble. He was good, and he was aware of it, but he was not content with that. He wanted everybody else to be good. I really believe that Wilkins could have carried on a Platonic love affair with an auburn-haired girl for ten weeks without an effort, he was so terribly good, which did not at all contribute to his popularity. A fellow who talks about ritualism while walking in the moonlight with a sentimental woman, doesn't count for much, and Wilkins was always doing things like that. It was even whispered last winter when he went sleigh-riding with that fascinating little widow, Mrs. Broughton, that he let her do the driving, clasped his own hands in front of him, and talked of nothing but the privations of the missionaries in China, and never mentioned oysters or cold birds and a bottle.

"And worst of all," snapped Mrs. Broughton, "he really seemed to enjoy it. I never saw such a man!"

I have mentioned all these details for the purpose of indicating how unpopular Wilkins was and how it was that he had become so, for with this knowledge the reader will share the surprise which we all felt when Wilkins suddenly blossomed forth as the most popular man of Dumfries Corners. It was really a knockdown blow to the most of us, for while we may have been jealous on occasions of each other, it never occurred to any of us to be jealous of the train-wrecker.

I didn't like it when Araminta smiled upon Harry Burnham, but it was not injurious to my self-respect that she should do it, because Harry Burnham averages up as good a fellow as I am, and then Harry and I could drown our differences in the flowing bowl later on. On the other hand, if Harry's Fiametta cast side glances at me, of course Harry would be wroth, but he could understand why Fiametta should be so affected by the twinkle in my eye—an affection by the way which has often got me unconsciously into trouble—that she should for the moment forget herself and respond to it.

But when Araminta and Fiametta on a sudden, just after the leap-year dance, wholly, and, as we thought, basely, deserted us for that emblem of conscious rectitude, Sam Wilkins, a man whose eye couldn't learn to twinkle in a thousand years, a mere human iceberg, then it was that we were astounded. Nor was this secession limited to Araminta and Fiametta. The conversion of the girls of Dumfries Corners to Wilkins was as complete, as comprehensive, as it was startling to the men. Jack Lester, as Bob Jenks expressed it, was "trun down" by Daisy Hawkins, who appeared to have eyes for none but Wilkins, while Bob, in turn, when going to make his usual Thursday evening call upon Miss Betsy Wilson, discovered that Miss Betsy had gone to the University extension lecture with the train-wrecker, an act unprecedented, for it had long been the custom for Bob to spend his Thursday evenings at the Wilson mansion, and, while nothing had as yet been announced, everybody in town was getting his congratulations ready for Bob as soon as that which was understood became a matter of common knowledge.

For a week or two we none of us let on that we had observed the remarkable change that had come o'er the spirit of our dreams. Harry has always been remarkable for his ability to conceal his feelings, and in that respect I am a good second, and except for the fact that we spent more time at the club playing pool nobody would have suspected that we cared whether Araminta or Fiametta still loved us or not. Besides, we each had a feeling that two could play at this Wilkins game, and I had made up my mind that if Araminta could so easily find a substitute for me I, with my twinkle, could as speedily replace her. That is to say, I felt that I could create that impression in

Araminta's mind, and that was all I was after. I didn't really intend, however easy it would be to do so, to create a flutter of a permanent nature in any other woman's heart—that is, not until I was sure that Araminta was lost to me forever. After a decent period of mourning I might have used my twinkle for permanent effect, but at that moment my only idea was to show Araminta that if one could be fickle, two could be twice as fickle. Harry had the same course of treatment in store for Fiametta, and we both made a strong bid for the company of Mary Brown, who, it must be confessed, was a charming girl, and stood second in the affections of every man in Dumfries Corners.

It was the opportunity of Mary Brown's life, for even as Harry and I had decided, so had all the other jilted swains, but that curious girl either could not or would not grasp it. She, too, had become a Wilkinsite, and would have nothing to do with any of us. She declined to attend the Beldens's musicale with me, and went bicycling with the iceberg. She told Robinson she hated lectures, and went to a stereopticon show with the train-wrecker. All the other men met with a similar rebuff, and at the last meeting of the Chafing Dish Club she capped the climax by refusing my lobster à la Newburg and Harry's oysters poulet, to have a second helping to the sole-leather welsh rarebit which Wilkins had constructed; Wilkins, a rank outsider, who had been asked to come to the meeting by every blessed girl in the club, although heretofore he had not been considered as a possible member, and in fact had been black-balled by the girls themselves! And when it came time for the girls to go home, instead of each one being escorted by a single male member, Wilkins corralled the whole lot of them in a huge omnibus which he had hired, and drove off with them, leaving us disconsolate. He smiled so broadly you could see his teeth in the dark.

This, as I have said, capped the climax.

"That settles it," said Burnham. "I'm going to New York for a rest. These Dumfries Corners girls needn't think they're the only women in the world. There are others."

"I'm going to stay and stick it out," said I. "I've got my sister left. She'll never succumb to the Wilkins influence."

But alas! I leaned upon a broken reed. My sister is a sensible girl, but she is "literary." She had a joke in *Life* once, and since that time she has neglected almost everything but writing and her brother. She doesn't neglect me, and altogether I'm glad she writes, since it fills her with enthusiasm until the articles come back, and up to now she had not written poetry. But, as I say, I leaned upon a broken reed, for when, the next day, I asked her what she was writing, she laughed and showed me a sonnet.

"Poetry, eh?" I said, disapprovingly, as I looked over her manuscript.

"Yes," she answered, modestly. "A sonnet."

And I read, "To S.W."

"Who's 'S.W.?'" I asked, with a frown, although I little suspected what her answer would be.

"Sam Wilkins," she replied.

I then realized the full force of Caesar's "Et tu, Brute?" and fled.

Meanwhile Wilkins was becoming insufferable. If Bunthorne was an ass, he was at least clever, but this Wilkins—he was a whole drove of asses, and not a redeeming feature to the lot. He could no more account for his sudden popularity than we could, but he could not help realizing it after a week or two, and then, for the first time in his life, he began to take notice. We men all wanted to thrash him, and I think Burnham would have done it if the rest of us hadn't prevented him.

"He needed a licking before this," said Harry, "but now he's worse than ever. It isn't conscious rectitude now, it's triumphant virtue. He makes me tired. He was telling me the other day that while girls might be captivated by flippant, superficial, prancing dudes for a while, in the end solid worth would win, and then he went on to say that the youth of modern times cultivated his feet to the exclusion of his head, and that while he had, of course, learned to dance, he had not devoted all his time to it, and regarded it, after all, as a very minor sort of an attraction as far as women are concerned. 'I don't rely on my dancing, Burnham,' he said. 'It's the head, and the heart, my boy, that triumphs.' And when I asked him where he learned all this he answered, 'from personal experience.'"

I immediately let go of Burnham. "Go and half-lick him, Harry," said I. "And when you've done with him pass him over to me, and I'll finish him. The supercilious ass."

That was the way Wilkins affected us.

The other men took their dose in different ways. Jenks began to drink a little more; Lester drank a little less. Hicks didn't care much about it one way or the other, and Wilson swore that if Wilkins came to call on his sister again he'd kick him out of the house.

Six weeks rolled by thus, and finally Easter Sunday came. No mitigation of the Wilkins visitation had entered into our lives. As the days wore on the girls became more devoted to him than ever, and he became correspondingly unbearable. The condescension with which he would treat his fellow-men was something hardly to be tolerated, and the worst of it was there didn't seem to be any way of bringing the girls to terms. There wasn't anybody left for us to flirt with now that Mary Brown had gone over to the enemy, she who had always been willing to flirt with anybody.

"There's only one hope," said Jenks. "If he'll only marry one of 'em, the others will come back. He can't marry 'em all, thank Heaven."

"Suppose it was Fiametta he married?" said I.

"Or Araminta!" was his preposterous retort.

"He'll never do that," said Lester. "He's in clover now, and for the first time in his life, and the more of an ass he is the more he'll like clover. He's paying attention to the lot. He'll never settle down to one. It's all up with us—unless he bankrupts himself."

"He won't," observed Harry Burnham. "Conscious rectitude won't do anything like that. I'm going to New York to call on an old flame, and I advise the rest of you to do the same."

"Well, I don't know but what you are right," said I, "but Araminta shall have one more chance. I'm going to church to-morrow. It's Easter Sunday, and I'll offer to escort her home. If she says 'yes,' all right. If she doesn't, I'm lost to her forever."

"Good scheme," quoth the others. "We're with you."

And that is what we all did. The girls were all there, resplendent in new bonnets and toggery of other sorts, and the smirking Wilkins was there too. He passed the plate after the sermon, and his rectitude shone out oleaginously on every line of his face. It was as much as I could do to keep from tripping him up in the aisle, and sending him and the contribution-plate sprawling. I almost did it when I imagined his feelings as the nickels rattled down through the register into the furnace below, but I restrained myself—and the killing glances he threw into those glass eyes of his, whenever he happened to hold the plate before one of those Dumfries girls! It was sickening, and I came near to flying before the close of the service. The others had the same sensations and temptations, and it is a wonder that Wilkins did not meet with some dreadful humiliation before he got the collection back into the chancel. It was a terrible strain on us, and his horrid unconsciousness that he was anything but perfect, and that the rest of us were anything more than so many paving stones to be walked on, was aggravating to a degree. Nothing unusual happened, however, and the service came to an end, and with it came to us all another surprise, but this time the surprise gave Wilkins a pain, and I had a front seat when the blow was dealt.

57

It had occurred to the immaculate rival of all the manhood of Dumfries Corners that he would honor Araminta with his society on the way home from church, and he and I reached her side after service at one and the same moment.

"May I have the pleasure of seeing you home?" said Wilkins, twirling his mustache with a "resist me if you can" smile on his lips.

"Don't let me interfere," said I, dryly, and was about to turn away.

"Thank you, Mr. Wilkins," replied Araminta, "but Mr. Smithers has already asked me."

It was a beautiful, lovely, sweet lie. I hadn't done anything of the sort, but I'd meant to, of course, and perhaps Araminta had become a mind reader. Wilkins got a little flushy around his cheek-bones, and posted off to Fiametta, but she and Burnham were already en route and apparently reconciled. So it went with all. Wilkins was left. Even my sister, who, lacking Wilkins, would have to walk home with the minister's wife, declined, and the fall of the great man was complete. Mary Brown was the only one remaining in the field, and when he fled to her she said she wasn't going home.

"Well, then," said Wilkins, "let me take you to wherever you are going?"

"Thank you," returned Miss Brown, "I'm not going there either," and she joined Araminta and myself, much to our delight, for we have no secrets from her. And then it all came out.

The girls had not loved us less, or Wilkins more, but they had resolved to keep Lent with unusual rigor this year.

*They had sworn us off and taken up Wilkins for penance.*

Hard on Wilkins?

Not a bit of it. He's as conscious of his rectitude and as unconscious of his unpopularity as ever.

Only he is a little more outspoken about women than he used to be, and somehow or other he has let it creep out that he "doesn't find them interesting."

"They can't even learn to dance without tripping a fellow up," says he.

# THE MAYOR'S LAMPS

The serpent had crept into Eden. The Perkins household for ten years had been little less than Paradise to its inmates, and then in a single night the reptile of political ambition had dragged his slimy length through those happy door-posts and now sat grinning indecently at the inscription over the library mantel, a ribbon mosaic bearing the sentiment "Here Dwells Content" let into the tiles thereof.

How it ever happened no man knoweth, but happen it did. Thaddeus Perkins was snatched from the arms of Peace and plunged headlong into the jaws of Political Warfare.

"They want me because they think I'm strong," he pleaded, in extenuation of his acceptance of the nomination for Mayor of his town.

"But you ought to know better," returned Mrs. Perkins, failing to realize what possible misconstruction her lord and master might put upon the answer. "The idea of your meddling in politics when you've got twice as much work as you can do already! I think it's awful!"

"I didn't seek it," he said, after hesitating a moment; "they've—they've thrust it on me." Then he tried to be funny. "With me, public office is a public thrust."

"Is there any salary?" asked Mrs. Perkins, treating the jest with the contempt it merited.

"No," said Thaddeus. "Not a cent; but—"

"Not a cent!" cried Mrs. Perkins. "And you are going to give up all your career, or at least two years of it, and probably the best two years of your life, for—"

"Glory," said Thaddeus.

"Glory! Humph," said Mrs. Perkins, "I am not aware that nations are talking of previous Mayors of Dumfries Corners. Mr. Jiggers's name is not a household word outside of this city, is it?"

Mr. Jiggers was the gentleman, into whose shoes Thaddeus was seeking to place his feet—the incumbent of the mighty office to which he aspired.

"Who is the present Lord Mayor of London?" the lady continued.

"Haven't the slightest idea," murmured the standard-bearer of the Democratic party, hopelessly.

"Or Berlin, or Peking—or even of Chicago?" she went on.

"What has that got to do with it?" retorted the worm, turning a trifle.

"You spoke of glory—the glory of being Mayor of Dumfries Corners, a city of 30,000 inhabitants. This is going to send your name echoing from sea to sea, reverberating through Europe, and thundering down through the ages to come; and yet you admit that the glories of the Mayors of London with 4,000,000 souls, of Berlin, Chicago, and Peking, with millions more, are so slight that you can't remember their names—or even to have heard them, for that matter. Really, Thaddeus, I am surprised at you. What you expect to get out of this besides nervous prostration I must confess I cannot see."

"Lamps," said Thaddeus, clutching like a drowning man at the one emolument of the coveted office.

Mrs. Perkins gazed at her husband anxiously. The answer was so unexpected and seemingly so absurd that she for a moment feared he had lost his mind. The notion that two years' service in so important an office as that of Mayor of Dumfries Corners received as its sole reward nothing but lamps was to her mind impossible.

"Is—is there anything the matter with you, dear?" she asked, placing her hand on his brow. "You don't seem feverish."

"Feverish?" snapped the leader of his party. "Who said anything about my being feverish?"

"Nobody, Teddy dear; but what you said about lamps made me think—made me think your mind was wandering a trifle."

"Oh—that!" laughed Perkins. "No, indeed—it's true. They always give the Mayor a pair of lamps. Some of them are very swell, too. You know those wrought-iron standards that Mr. Berkeley has in front of his place?"

"The ones at the driveway entrance, on the bowlders?"

"Yes."

"They're beauties. I've always admired those lamps very much."

"Well—they are the rewards of Mr. Berkeley's political virtue. I paid for them, and so did all the rest of the tax-payers. They are his Mayor's lamps, and if I'm elected I'll have a pair just like them, if I want them like that."

"Oh, I do hope you'll get in, Teddy," said the little woman, anxiously, after a reflective pause. "They'd look stunning on our gate-posts."

"I don't think I shall have them there," said Thaddeus. "Jiggers has the right idea, seems to me—he's put 'em on the newel-posts of his front porch steps."

"I don't suppose they'd give us the money and let us buy one handsome cloisonné lamp from Tiffany's, would they?" Mrs. Perkins asked.

"A cloisonné lamp on a gate-post?" laughed Perkins.

"Of course not," rejoined the lady. "You know I didn't mean any such thing. I saw a perfectly beautiful lamp in Tiffany's last Wednesday, and it would go so well in the parlor—"

"That wouldn't be possible, my dear," said Thaddeus, still smiling. "You don't quite catch the idea of those lamps. They're sort of like the red, white, and blue lights in a drug-store window in intention. They are put up to show the public that that is where a political prescription for the body politic may be compounded. The public is responsible for the bills, and the public expects to use what little light can be extracted from them."

"Then all this generosity on the public's part is—"

"Merely that of the Indian who gives and takes back," said Thaddeus.

"And they must be out-of-doors?" asked Mrs. Perkins. "If I set the cloisonné lamp in the window, it wouldn't do?"

"No," said Thaddeus. "They must be out-of-doors."

"Well, I hope the nasty old public will stay there too, and not come traipsing all over my house," snapped Mrs. Perkins, indignantly.

And then for a little time the discussion of the Mayor's lamps stopped.

The campaign went on, and Thaddeus night after night was forced to go out to speak here and there and everywhere. One night he travelled five miles through mud and rain to address an organization of tax-payers, and found them assembled before the long mahogany counter of a beer-saloon, which was the "Hall" they had secured for the reception of the idol of their hopes; and among them it is safe to say there was not one who ever saw a tax-bill, and not many who knew more about those luxuries of life than the delicious flunky, immortalized by Mr. Punch, who says to a brother flunky, "I say, Tummas, wot is taxes?" And he told them his principles and promised to do his best for them, and bade them good-night, and went away leaving them parched and dry and downcast. And then the other fellow came, and won their hearts and "set them up again." Another night he attended another meeting and lost a number of friends because he shone at both ends but not in the middle. If he had taken a glittering coin or two from his vest-pocket on behalf of the noble working-men there assembled in great numbers and spirituous mood, they would have forgiven him his wit and patent-leather shoes—and so it went. Perkins was nightly hauled hither and yon by the man he called his "Hagenbeck," the manager of the wild animal he felt himself gradually degenerating into, and his wife and home and children saw less of him than of the unimportant floating voter whose mind was open to conviction, but could be reached only by way of the throat.

"Two o'clock last night; one o'clock the night before; I suppose it'll be three before you are in to-night?" Mrs. Perkins said, ruefully.

"I do not know, my dear," replied Thaddeus. "There are five meetings on for to-night."

"Well, I think they ought to give you the lamps now," said Mrs. Perkins. "It seems to me this is when you need them most."

"True," said Thaddeus, sadly, for in his secret soul he was beginning to be afraid he would be elected; and now that he saw what kind of people Mayors have to associate with, the glory of it did not seem to be worth the cost. "I'm a sort of Night-Mayor just at present, and those lamps would come in handy in the wee sma' hours," he groaned. And then he sighed and pined for the peaceful days of yore when he was content to walk his ways with no nation upon his shoulders.

"I never envied Atlas anyhow," he confided to himself later, as he tossed about upon his bed and called himself names. "It always seemed to me that this revolving globe must rub the skin off his neck and back; but now, poor devil, with just one municipality hanging over me, I can appreciate more than ever the difficulties of his position—except that he doesn't have to make speeches to 'tax-payers.' Humph! Taxpayers! It's tax-makers. If I'd promised to go into all sorts of wilderness improvement for the sole and only purpose of putting these 'tax-payers' on the corporation at the expense of real laboring-men, I'd win in a canter."

"What is the matter, Thaddeus?" said Mrs. Perkins, coming in from the other room. "Can't you sleep?"

"Don't want to sleep, my dear," returned the candidate. "When I go to sleep I dream I'm addressing mass-meetings. I can't enjoy my rest unless I stay awake. Did your mother come to-day?"

"Yes—and, oh, she's so enthusiastic, Teddy!"

"At last! About me? You don't mean it."

"No—about the lamps. She says lamps are just what we need to complete the entrance. She thinks Mr. Berkeley's scheme of putting them on the stone posts is the best. There's more dignity about it. Putting them on the piazza steps, she says, looks ostentatious, and suggests a beer-saloon or a road-house."

"Well, my dear, that's about all politics seems to amount to," said the reformer. "If those lamps are to be a souvenir of the campaign, they ought to suggest road-houses and beer-saloons."

"They will not be souvenirs of a campaign," replied Mrs. Perkins, proudly. "They will be the outward and visible sign of my husband's merit; the emblem of victory."

"The red badge of triumph, eh?" smiled the candidate, wanly. "Well, my dear, have them where you please, and keep them well filled with alcohol, even if they do burn gas. They'll represent the tax-payers when they get that."

"You musn't get so tired, Thaddeus dear," said the little woman, smoothing his forehead soothingly with her hand. "You seem unusually tired to-night."

"I am," said Thaddeus, shortly. "The debate wore me out."

"Did you debate? I thought you said you wouldn't."

"Well, I did. Everybody said I was afraid to meet Captain Haskins on the platform, so we had it out to-night over in the Tenth Ward. I talked for sixty-eight minutes, gave 'em my views, and then he got up."

"What did he say. Could he answer you?"

"No—but he won the day. All he said was: 'Well, boys, I'm not much of a talker, but I'll say one thing—Perkins, while my adversary, is still my friend, and I'm proud of him. Now, if you'll all join me at the bar, we'll drink his health—on me.'" Thaddeus paused, and then he added: "I imagine they're cheering yet; at any rate, if I have as much health as they drink—on Haskins —I'll double discount old Methuselah in the matter of years."

The next morning at breakfast the pale and nervous standard-bearer was affectionately greeted by his mother-in-law.

"I've been thinking about those lamps all night," she said, after a few minutes. "The trouble about the gate-posts is that you have three gate-posts and only two lamps."

"Maybe they'd let us buy three lamps instead of two," suggested Mrs. Perkins.

"Well, we won't, even if they do let us," observed Perkins, with some irritation. He had just received a newspaper from a kind friend in Massachusetts with a comic biography and dissipated wood-cut of himself in it. "I'm not starting a concert-hall, and I'm not going to put a row of lamps along the front of my place."

"I quite agree with you," replied his mother-in-law. "It occurred to me we might put them, like hanging lanterns, on each of the chimneys. It would be odd."

Thaddeus muttered two syllables to himself, the latter of which sounded like M'dodd, but exactly what it was he said I can only guess. Then he added: "They won't go there. I can't get a gas-pipe up through those chimneys. It's as much as we can do to get the smoke up, much less a gas-pipe. Even if we got the gas-pipe through, it wouldn't do. A putty-blower would choke up the flues."

"Well, I don't know," said the mother-in-law, placidly. "It seems to me—"

A glance from Mrs. Perkins stopped the dear old lady. I think Mrs. Perkins's sympathetic disposition taught her that her husband was having a hard time being agreeable, and that further discussion of the lamp question was likely to prove disastrous.

Thaddeus was soon called for by his manager, and started out to meet the leading lights of the Hungarian and Italian quarters. The Germans had been made solid the day before, and as for the Irish, they were supposed to be with Perkins on principle, because Perkins was not in accord politically with the existing administration.

"It's too bad he's so nervous," said his mother-in-law, as he went out.

"They say women are nervous, but I must say I don't think much of the endurance of men. How absurd he was when he spoke of the gas-pipe through the chimney!"

"Well, I suppose, my dear mother," said Mrs. Perkins, sadly—"I suppose he can't be bothered with little details like the lamps now. There are other questions to be considered."

"What is the exact issue?" asked the mother-in-law, interestedly. "Well—

the tariff, and—ah—and taxes, and—ah—money, and—ah—ah—I think the saloon question enters in somehow. I believe Mr. Haskins wants more of them, and Thaddeus says there are too many of them as it is. And now they are both investigating them, I fancy, because Teddy was in one the other day."

"We ought to help him a little," said the elder woman. "Let's just relieve him of the whole lamp question; decide where to put them, go to New York and pick them out, get estimates for the laying of the pipes, and surprise him by having them all ready to put up the day after election."

"Wouldn't it be fun!" cried Mrs. Perkins, delightedly. "He'll be so surprised —poor dear boy. I'll do it. I'll send down this morning for Mr. O'Hara to come up here and see how we can make the connection and where the trenches for the pipes can be laid. Mr. O'Hara is the best-known contractor in town, and I guess he's the man we want."

And immediately O'Hara was telephoned for to come up to Mr. Perkins's, and the fair conspirators were not aware of, and probably will never realize, the importance politically of that act. Mr. O'Hara refused to come, but it was hinted about that Perkins had summoned him, and there was great joy among the rank and file, and woe among the better elements, for O'Hara was a boss, and a boss whose power was one of the things Thaddeus was trying to break, and the cohorts fancied that the apostle of purity had realized that without O'Hara reform was fallen into the pit. Furthermore, as cities of the third class, like Dumfries Corners, live conversationally on rumors and gossipings, it was not an hour before almost all Dumfries Corners, except Thaddeus Perkins himself and his manager, knew that the idol had bowed before the boss's hat, and that the boss had returned the grand message that he'd see Perkins in the Hudson River before he'd go to his damned mugwump temple; and in two hours they also knew it, for they heard in no uncertain terms from the secretary of the Municipal Club, a reform organization, which had been instrumental in securing Perkins's nomination, who demanded to know in an explicit yes or no as to whether any such message had been sent. The denial was made, and then the lie was given; and many to this day wonder exactly where the truth lay. At any rate, votes were lost and few gained, and many a worthy friend of good government lost heart and bemoaned the degeneration of the gentleman into the politician.

Perkins, worn out, irritated by, if not angry at, what he termed the underhanded lying of the opposition, drove home for luncheon, and found his wife and her mother in a state of high dudgeon. They had been insulted.

"It was frightful the language that man used, Thaddeus," said Mrs. Perkins.

"He wouldn't have dared do it except by telephone," put in the mother-in-law, whose notions were somewhat old-fashioned. "I've always hated that machine. People can lie to you and you can't look 'em in the eye over it, and they can say things to your face with absolute opportunity."

The dear old lady meant impunity, but it must be remembered that she was excited.

"Well, I think he ought to be chastised," said Mrs. Perkins.

"Who? What are you talking about?" demanded Thaddeus.

"That nasty O'Hara man," said Mrs. Perkins. "He said 'he'd be damned' over the wire."

Thaddeus immediately became energetic. "He didn't blackguard you, did he?" he demanded.

"Yes, he did," said Mrs. Perkins, the water in her eyes affecting her voice so that it became mellifluous instead of merely melodious.

"But how?" persisted Perkins.

"Well—we—we—rang him up—it was only as a surprise, you know, dear

—we rang him up—"

"You—you rang up—O'Hara?" cried Perkins, aghast. "It must have been a surprise."

"Yes, Teddy. We were going to settle the lamp question; we thought you were bothered enough with—well, with affairs of state—"

The candidate drew up proudly, but immediately became limp again as he realized the situation.

"And," Mrs. Perkins continued, "we thought we'd relieve you of the lamp question; and as Mr. O'Hara is a great contractor—the most noted in all Dumfries Corners—isn't he?"

"Yes, yes, yes! he is!" said Perkins, furiously; "but what of that?"

"Well, that's why we rang him up," said Mrs. Perkins, with a sigh of relief to find that she had selected the right man. "We wanted Mr. O'Hara to dig the trench for the pipes, and lay the pipes—"

"He's a great pipe-layer!" ejaculated Perkins.

"Exactly," rejoined Mrs. Perkins, solemnly. "We'd heard that, and so we asked him to come up."

"But, my dear," cried Perkins, dismayed, "you didn't tell him you wanted him to put up my lamps? I'm not elected yet."

The agony of the moment for Perkins can be better imagined than portrayed.

"He didn't give us the chance," said the mother-in-law. "He merely swore."

Perkins drew a sigh of relief. He understood it all now, and in spite of the position in which he was placed he was glad. "Jove!" he said to himself, "it was a narrow escape. Suppose O'Hara had come! He'd have enjoyed laying pipes for a Mayor's lamps for me—two weeks before election."

And for the first time in weeks Perkins was faintly mirthful. The narrowness of his escape had made him hysterical, and he actually indulged in the luxury of a nervous laugh.

"That accounts for the rumor," he said to himself, and then his heart grew heavy again. "The rumor is true, and—Oh, well, this is what I get for dabbling in politics. If I ever get out of this alive, I vow by all the gods politics shall know me no more."

"It was all right—my asking O'Hara, Thaddeus?" asked Mrs. Perkins.

"Oh yes, certainly, my dear—perfectly right. O'Hara is indeed, as you thought, the most noted, not to say notorious, contractor in town, only he's not laying pipes just now. He's pulling wires."

"For telephones, I presume?" said the old lady, placidly.

"Well, in a way," replied Thaddeus. "There's a great deal of vocality about O'Hara's wires. But, Bess," he added, seriously, "just drop the lamps until we get 'em, and confine your telephoning to your intimate friends. An Irishman on a telephone in political times is apt to be a trifle—er—artless in his choice of words. If you must talk to one of 'em, remember to put in the lightning plug before you begin."

With which injunction the candidate departed to address the Mohawks, an independent political organization in the Second Ward, which was made up of thinking men who never indorsed a candidate without knowing why, and rarely before three o'clock of the afternoon of election day at that, by whom he was received with cheers and back-slapping and button-holings which convinced him that he was the most popular man on earth, though on election day—but election day has yet to be described. It came, and with it there came to Perkins a feeling very much like that which the small boy experiences on the day before Christmas. He has been good for two months, and he knows that to-morrow the period of probation will be over and he can be as bad as he pleases again for a little while anyhow.

"However it turns out, I can tell 'em all to go to the devil to-morrow," chuckled Thaddeus, rubbing his hands gleefully.

"I don't think you ought to forget the lamps, Thaddeus," observed the mother-in-law at breakfast. "Here it is election day and you haven't yet decided where they shall go. Now I really think—"

"Never mind the lamps," returned Thaddeus. "Let's talk of ballot-boxes to-day. To-morrow we can place the lamps."

"Very well, if you say so," said the old lady; "only I marvel at you latter-day boys. In my young days a small matter like that would have been settled long ago."

"Well, I'll compromise with you," said

Thaddeus. "We won't wait until to-morrow. I'll decide the question to-night —I'm really too busy now to think of them."

"I shall be glad when we don't have to think about 'em at all," sighed Mrs. Perkins, pouring out the candidate's coffee. "They've really been a care to me. I don't like the idea of putting them on the porch, or on the gate-posts either. They'll have to be kept clean, and goodness knows I can't ask the girls to go out in the middle of winter to clean them if they are on the gate-posts."

"Mike will clean them," said Thaddeus.

Mrs. Perkins sniffed when Mike's name was mentioned. "I doubt it," she said. "He's been lots of good for two weeks."

"Mike has been lots of good for two weeks," echoed Thaddeus, enthusiastically. "He's kept all the hired men in line, my dear."

"I've no doubt he's been of use politically, but from a domestic point of view he's been awful. He's been drunk for the last week."

"Well, my love," said the candidate, despairingly, "some member of the family had to be drunk for the last week, and I'd rather it was Mike than you or any of the children. Mike's geniality has shed a radiance about me among the hired men of this town that fills me with pride."

"I don't see, to go back to what I said in the very beginning, why we can't have the lamps in-doors," returned Mrs. Perkins.

"I told you why not, my dear," said Perkins. "They are the perquisite of the Mayor, but for the benefit of the public, because the public pays for them."

"And hasn't the public, as you call it, taken possession of the inside of your house?" demanded the mother-in-law. "I found seven gentlemen sitting in the white and gold parlor only last night, and they hadn't wiped their feet either."

"You don't understand," faltered the standard-bearer. "That business isn't permanent. To-morrow I'll tell them to go round to the back door and ask the cook."

"Humph!" said the mother-in-law. "I'm surprised at you. For a few paltry votes you—"

Just here the front door bell rang, and the business of the day beginning stopped the conversation, which bade fair to become unpleasant.

---

Night came. The votes were being counted, and at six o'clock Perkins was informed that everything was going his way.

"Get your place ready for a brass band and a serenade," his manager telephoned.

"I sha'n't!" ejaculated the candidate to himself, his old-time independence asserting itself now that the polls were closed—and he was right. He didn't have to. The band did not play in his front yard, for at eight o'clock the tide that had set in strong for Perkins turned. At ten, according to votes that had been counted, things were about even, and the ladies retired. At twelve Perkins turned out the gas.

"That settles the lamp question, anyhow," he whispered to himself as he went up-stairs, and then he went into Mrs. Perkins's room.

"Well, Bess," he said, "it's all over, and I've made up my mind as to where the lamps are to go."

"Good!" said the little woman. "On the gate-posts?"

"No, dear. In the parlor—the cloisonné lamps from Tiffany's."

"Why, I thought you said we couldn't—"

"Well, we can. Our lamps can go in there whether the public likes it or not. We are emancipated."

"But I don't understand," began Mrs. Perkins.

"Oh, it's simple," said Thaddeus, with a sigh of mingled relief and chagrin. "It's simple enough. The other lamps are to be put—er—on Captain Haskins's place."

---

# THE BALANCE OF POWER

It was a pleasant night in the spring of 189-.

The residents of Dumfries Corners were enjoying an early spring, and suffering from the demoralizing influences of a municipal election. Incidentally Mr. Thaddeus Perkins, candidate, was beginning to feel very much like Moses when he saw the promised land afar. The promised land was now in plain sight; but whether or not the name of Perkins should be inscribed in one of its high places depended upon the voters who on the morrow were to let their ballots express their choice as to who should preside over the interests of the city and hold in check the fiery, untamed aldermen of Dumfries Corners.

The candidate was tired, very tired, and was trying to gain a few hours' rest before plunging again and for the last time into the whirlpool of vote-getting; and as he sat enjoying a few moments of blissful ease behind the close-drawn portieres of his library there came the much-dreaded sound of heavy feet upon the porch without, and the door-bell rang.

"Norah!" cried the candidate, in an agonized stage-whisper, as the maid approached in answer to the summons, "tell them I'm out, unless it's some one of my personal friends."

"Yis, sorr," was the answer. "Oi will."

And the door was opened.

"Is Misther Perkins in?" came a deep, unmistakably "voting" voice from without.

"Oi dun'no'. Are yees a personal friend of Misther Perkins?" was the response, and the heart of the listening Perkins sought his boots.

"Oi am not, but—" said the deep voice.

"Thin he isn't in," said Norah, positively.

"When 'll he be back?" asked the visitor, huskily.

"Ye say ye niver met him?" demanded Norah.

"Oi told ye oi hadn't," said the visitor, a trifle irritably. "But—"

"Thin he'll niver be back," put in the glorious Norah, and she shut the door with considerable force and retired.

For a moment the candidate was overcome; first he paled, but then catching Mrs. Perkins's eye and noting a twinkle of amusement therein, he yielded to his emotions and roared with laughter. What if Norah's manner was unconventional? Had she not carried out instructions?

"My dear," said the candidate to Mrs. Perkins, as the shuffling feet on the porch shuffled off into the night, "what wages do you pay Norah?"

"Sixteen dollars, Thaddeus," was the answer. "Why?"

"Make it twenty hereafter," replied the candidate. "She is an emerald beyond price. If I had only let her meet the nominating committee when they entered our little Eden three weeks ago, I should not now be involved in this wretched game of politics."

"Well, I sincerely wish you had," Mrs. Perkins observed, heartily. "This affair has made a very different man of you, and as for your family, they hardly see you any more. You are neglecting every single household duty for your horrid old politics."

"Well, now, my dear—" began the candidate.

"The pipes in the laundry have been leaking for four days now, and yet you won't send for a plumber, or even let me send for one," continued Mrs. Perkins.

"Well, Bessie dear, how can I? The race is awfully close. It wouldn't surprise me if the majority either way was less than a hundred."

"There you go again, Thaddeus. What on earth has the leak in the laundry pipes to do with the political situation?" asked the puzzled woman.

The candidate showed that in spite of his recent affiliations he still retained some remnant of his former self-respect, for he blushed as he thought of the explanation; but he tried nevertheless to shuffle out of it.

"Of course you can't understand," he said, with a cowardly resolve to shirk the issue. "That's because you are a woman, Bess. Women don't understand great political questions. And what I have particularly liked about you is that you never pretended that you did."

"Well, I'd like to know," persisted Mrs. Perkins. "I want to be of as much assistance to my husband in his work as I can, and if public questions are hereafter to be the problems of your life, they must become my problems too. Besides, my curiosity is really aroused in this especial case, and I'd love to know what bearing our calling a plumber has upon the tariff, or the money question, or any other thing in politics."

The candidate hesitated. He was cornered, and he did not exactly like the prospect.

"Well—" he began. "You see, I'm standing as the representative of a great party, and we—we naturally wish to win. If I am defeated, every one will say that it is a rebuke to the administration at Washington; and so, you see, we'd better let those leaks leak until day after to-morrow, when the voting will all be over."

Mrs. Perkins looked at her husband narrowly.

"I think I'll have to call the doctor," was her comment. "Either for you or for myself, Teddy. One of us is gone—wholly gone, mentally. There's no question about it, either you are rambling in your speech, or I have entirely lost all comprehension of the English language."

"I don't see—" began Perkins.

"Neither do I," interrupted Mrs. Perkins; "and I hardly hope to. You've explained and explained, but how a plumber's calling here to fix a laundry leak is to rebuke the administration at Washington is still far beyond me."

"But the plumbers are said to hold the balance of power!" cried the candidate. "There are a hundred of them here in Dumfries Corners, and each one controls at least five assistants, which makes six hundred voters in all. If I call in one, he and his five workers will vote for me, but the other five hundred and ninety-four will vote for Haskins; and if they do, the administration might as well go out of business. Can't you see? It's the same with the dandelions. These spring elections are perfect—ah—Gehenna for a candidate if it happens to be an early spring like this."

Perkins's voice had the suggestion of a wail in it as he spoke of the dandelions, and his wife's alarm grew upon her. She understood now about the plumber, but his interjection of the dandelions had brought a fearful doubt into her heart. Surely he was losing his mind.

"Dandelions, Thaddeus?" she echoed, aghast.

"Yes, dandelions," retorted the candidate, forcibly. "They've queered me as much as anything. The neighbors say I'm not a good neighbor because I don't have them pulled. Mike's been so thoroughly alcoholic all through the fight, looking after my interests, that he can't pull them; and if I hire two men to come and do the work, seven hundred other men will want to know why they didn't get a chance."

"But why not employ boys?" demanded Mrs. Perkins.

"And be set down as an advocate of cheap child labor? Not I!" cried Perkins.

"Then the dandelion-pullers are another balance of power, are they?" asked Mrs. Perkins, beginning to grow somewhat easier in her mind as to her husband's sanity.

"Precisely; you have a very remarkable gift of insight, Bess," answered the candidate.

"And how many balances of power are there?" demanded the lady.

"The Lord only knows," sighed Perkins. "I've made about eighty of 'em solid already, but as soon as one balance is fixed a thousand others rise up like Banquo's ghost, and will not down. I haven't a doubt that it was a balance of power that Norah just turned away from the front door. They strike you everywhere. Why, even Bobbie ruined me with one of them in the Eighth Ward the other day—one solidified balance wiped out in a moment by my interesting son."

"Bobbie?" cried Mrs. Perkins. "A six-year-old boy?"

"Exactly—Bobbie, the six-year-old boy. I wish you'd keep the children in the house until this infernal business is over. The Eighth Ward would have elected me; but Bobbie ruined that," said Perkins, ruefully.

"But how?" cried Mrs. Perkins. "Have our children been out making campaign speeches for the other side?"

"They have," assented Perkins. "They have indeed. You remember that man Jorrigan?"

"The striker?" queried Mrs. Perkins, calling to mind a burly combination of red hair and bad manners who had made himself very conspicuous of late.

"Precisely. That's just the point," retorted Perkins. "The striker. That's what he is, and it's what you call him."

"But you said he was a striker at breakfast last Wednesday," said Mrs. Perkins. "We simply take your word for it."

"I know I did. He's also a balance of power, my dear. Jorrigan controls the Eighth Ward. That's the only reason I've let him in the house," said Thaddeus.

"You've been very chummy with him, I must say," sniffed Mrs. Perkins.

"Well, I've had to be," said the candidate. "That man is a power, and he knows it."

"What's his business?" asked Mrs. Perkins.

"Interference between capital and labor," replied Perkins. "So I've cultivated him."

"He never struck me as being a very cultivated person," smiled Mrs. Perkins. "He has a suggestion of alcohol about him that is very oppressive."

"I know—he has a very intoxicating presence," said the candidate, joining in the smile. "But we are rid of his presence now and forever, thanks to Bobbie. I got the news last night. He and his followers have declared for Haskins, in spite of all his promises to me, and we can attribute our personal good fortune and our political loss to Bobbie. Bobbie met him on the street the other day."

"I know he did," said Mrs. Perkins. "He told me so, and he said that the horrid man wanted to kiss him."

"It's true," said Perkins. "He did, and Bobbie wouldn't let him."

"Well, a man isn't going back on you because he can't kiss your whole family, is he?" asked Mrs. Perkins, apprehensively. "If that's the situation, I shall go to New York to-morrow."

Perkins laughed heartily. "No, my dear," he said. "You are safe enough from that. But Jorrigan, when Bobbie refused, said, 'Well, young feller, I guess you don't know who I am?' 'Yes, I do,' said Bobbie. 'You are Mr. Jorrigan,' and Jorrigan was overjoyed; but Bobbie destroyed his good work by adding, 'Jorrigan the striker,' and the striker's joy vanished. 'Who told you that?' said he. 'Pop—and he knows,' said Bobbie. That night," continued Perkins, with a droll expression of mingled mirth and annoyance, "the amalgamated mortar-mixers of the Eighth Ward decided that consideration for the country's welfare should rise above partisan politics, and that when it came to real statesmanship Haskins could give me points. A ward wiped out in a night, and another highly interesting, very thirsty balance of power gone over to the other side."

"I should think you'd give up, then," said Mrs. Perkins, despairfully. She wanted her husband to win—not because she had any ambition to shine as "Lady-Mayor," but because she did not wish Thaddeus to incur disappointment or undergo the chagrin of a public rebuke. "You seem to be losing balances of power right and left."

"Why should I give it up?" queried Perkins. "You don't suppose I am having any better luck than Mr. Haskins, do you?"

"Is he losing them too?" asked Mrs. Perkins, hopefully.

"I judge so from what he tells me," said Perkins. "We took dinner together at the Centurion in New York the other night, and he's a prince of good fellows, Bess. He has just as much trouble as I have, and when I met him on the train the other day he was as blue as I about the future."

"You and the captain dining together?" ejaculated Mrs. Perkins.

"Certainly," said Perkins. "Why not? Our hatred is merely political, and we can meet on a level of good-fellowship anywhere outside of Dumfries Corners."

Mrs. Perkins laughed outright. "Isn't it funny!" she said.

"Why, Haskins is one of my best friends, generally," continued Perkins. "I don't see anything funny about it. Just because we both happen to be dragged into politics on opposite sides at the same moment is no reason why we should begin cutting each other's throats, my dear. In fact, with balances of power springing up all over town like mushrooms, we have become companions in misery."

"Well, I don't see why you can't get together, then, and tell these balances to go to—to grass," suggested Mrs. Perkins.

"Grass is too mild, my love," remarked the candidate, smiling quietly. "They wouldn't go there, even if we told them to, so it would be simply a waste of breath. We've got to grin and bear them until the polls close, and then we can pitch in and tell 'em what we think of them."

"Just the same," continued Mrs. Perkins, "an agreement between Mr. Haskins and you to ignore these people utterly, instead of taking them into your family, would stop the whole abuse."

"That's a woman's idea," said Perkins, bravely, though in the innermost recesses of his heart he wished he had thought of it before. "It isn't practical politics, my love. You might as well say that two opposing generals in a war could save thousands of lives by avoiding each other's armies and keeping out of a fight."

"Well, I do say that," replied Mrs.

Perkins, positively. "That's exactly my view of what generals ought to do."

"And what would become of the war?" queried the candidate.

"There wouldn't be any," said the good little woman.

"Precisely," retorted Perkins. "Precisely. And if Haskins and I did what you want us to do, there would be no more politics."

"Well, what of it?" demanded Mrs. Perkins. "Are politics the salvation of the country? It's as bad as war."

"Humph!" grunted Perkins. "It is difficult to please women. You hate war because, to settle a question of right, people go out into the field of battle and mow each other down with guns; you cry for arbitration. Let all questions, all differences of opinion, be settled by a resort to reason, say you—which is beautiful, and undoubtedly proper. But when we try to settle our differences by a bloodless warfare, in which the ballot is one's ammunition, you cry down with politics. A political contest is nothing but a bit of supreme arbitration, for which you peace people are always clamoring, by the court of last resort, the people."

Mrs. Perkins smiled sweetly, and taking her husband's hand in hers, stroked it softly.

"Teddy dear, you mustn't be so politic with me," she said; "I'm not a campaign club. I know that sentiment you have just expressed is lofty and noble, and ought to be true, and I know we used to think it was true—three weeks ago I believed it when you said it; but this is now, dear. This is to-night, not three weeks ago, and I have changed my mind."

"Well," began the candidate, hesitatingly, "I don't know but that I am weakening a trifle myself."

"I know," interposed Mrs. Perkins, "you are weakening. You know as well as I do that the hard work you are doing is not in appealing to the reason of the supreme court of arbitration, the people. You are appealing, as you have said, yourself, to a large and interesting variety of balances of power, that do not want your views or your opinions or your arguments, but they do want your money to buy cigars and beer with. They want you to buy their good-will; and even if you bought it, I doubt if they would concede to you a controlling interest in it if Mr. Haskins should happen to want some of it, and I don't doubt he does."

"You don't know anything—" the candidate ventured.

"Yes I do, too," returned Mrs. Perkins, with the self-satisfied nod which the average new woman gives when she thinks she is right, though Mrs. Perkins had no pretensions in that direction, happily for her family. "I know all that you have told me. I know that when you were to dine at Colonel Buckley's on Wednesday night you wore your evening dress, and that when leaving there early to go to the city and address the Mohawk Independent Club you asked your manager if you could go dressed as you were, and his answer was, 'Not on your life,' and you went home and put on your business suit. You told me that yourself, and yet you talk about the supreme court of arbitration, the people!"

"But, Bess, the Mohawks are a powerful organization," pleaded Perkins. "I couldn't afford to offend them."

"No. It was the first balance of power that turned up. I remember it well. It was to be convinced by arguments. You were going down there to discuss principles, but you couldn't appeal to their judicial minds or reach their reason unless you changed your clothes; and when you got there as their guest, and ventured to ask for a glass of Vichy before you spoke, do you remember what they brought you?" demanded Mrs. Perkins, warming up to her subject.

The candidate smiled faintly. "Yes," he answered. "Beer."

"Exactly; and when he gave you the beer, that MacHenty man whispered in your ear, 'Drink that; it'll go better wid the byes.'"

"He did," said Thaddeus, meekly.

"And yet you talk about this appeal to a reasonable balance of power! Really, Teddy, you are becoming demoralized. Politics, as I see it, is an appeal to thirst, and nothing else."

"'You never miss the voter till the keg runs dry,'" sang the candidate, with a more or less successful attempt at gayety. "But never mind, Bess. I've had enough, and if I'm beaten this time I'll never do it again. So don't worry; and, after all, this is only a municipal election.

The difference between a grand inspiring massive war for principle and a street riot. The supreme court of arbitration, the people, can be relied on to do the right thing in the end. They are sane. They are honest. They are not all thirsty, and in this as in all contests the blatant attract the most attention. The barker at the door of the side show to the circus makes more noise than the eight-headed boy that makes the mare go."

"You're a trifle mixed in your metaphors, Teddy," said Mrs. Perkins.

"Well who wouldn't be, after a three weeks' appeal to an arid waste of voters?"

"A waste of arid voters," amended Mrs. Perkins.

"The amendment is accepted," laughed Thaddeus. And at that moment a telephone call from headquarters summoned him abroad.

"Good-night, Bess," he said, kissing his wife affectionately. "This is the last night."

"Good-night, Teddy; I hope it is. And next time when they ask you to run —"

"You shall be the balance of power, and decide the question for me," said the candidate, as, with sorrow in his heart, he left his home to seek out what he called "the branch office of Hades," political headquarters, where were gathered some fifty persons, most of whom began life in other countries, under different skies, and to whom the national anthem "America" meant less and aroused fewer sentiments worth having than that attractive two-step "St. Patrick's Day in the Morning," and who were yet sufficiently powerful with the various "balances" of the town to hold its political destinies in their itching palms.

---

Two months after this discussion the late Honorable Thaddeus Perkins, ex-candidate, and Mayor of Dumfries Corners only by courtesy of those who honor defeated candidates with titles for which they have striven unsuccessfully, was strolling through the country along the line of the Croton Aqueduct, trying to disentangle, with the aid of the fresh sweet air of an early summer afternoon, an idea for a sonnet from the mazes of his brain. Stopping for a moment to look down upon the glorious Hudson stretching its shimmering length like a bimetallic serpent to the north and south, he suddenly became conscious of a pair of very sharp eyes resting upon him, which a closer inspection showed belonged to a laborer of seemingly diminutive stature, who was engaged in carrying earth in a wheelbarrow from one dirt-pile to another. As Thaddeus caught his eye the laborer assumed towering proportions. He rose up quite two feet higher in the air and bowed.

"How do you do?" said Perkins, returning the salutation courteously, wondering the while as to what might be the cause of this sudden change of height.

"Oi'm well—which is nothin' new to me," replied the other. "Ut sheems to me," he continued, "thot youse resimbles thot smart young felly Perkins, the Mayor of Dumfries Corners—not!"

Perkins laughed. The sting of defeat had lost its power to annoy, and his experience had become merely one of a thousand other nightmares of the past.

"Do I?" he replied, resolving not to confess his identity, for the moment at least.

"Only thinner," chuckled the laborer, shrinking up again; and Perkins now saw that the legs of his new acquaintance were of an abnormally unequal length, which forced him every time he shifted his weight from one foot to the other to change his apparent height to a startling degree. "An' a gude dale thinner," he repeated. "There's nothin' loike polithical exersoize to take off th' flesh, parthicularly when ye miss ut."

"I fancy you are right," said Perkins. "I never met Mr. Perkins—that is, face to face—myself. Do you know him?"

The Irishman threw his head back and laughed.

"Well," he said, "oi'm not wan uv his pershonal fri'nds. But oi know um when oi see um," and he looked Thaddeus straight in the eye as he grew tall again.

"I'm sure it is Perkins's loss," returned Thaddeus, "that you are not a personal friend of his."

"It was," said the Irishman. "My name is Finn," he added, with an air which seemed to assume that Perkins would begin to tremble at the dreaded word; but Perkins did not tremble. He merely replied,

"A very good name, Mr. Finn."

"Oi t'ink so," assented Mr. Finn. "Ut's better nor Dinnis, me young fri'nd."

Perkins assented to this proposition as though it was merely general, and had no particular application to the affairs of the moment. "I suppose, Mr. Finn," he observed, shortly, "that you were one of the earnest workers in the late campaign for Mr. Perkins?"

"Was he elicted?" asked Finn, scornfully.

"I believe not," began Thaddeus. "But—"

"Thot's me answer to your quistion, sorr," said Finn, with dignity. "He'd 'a' had lamps befoor his house now, sorr, if he hadn't been gay wid his front dure."

"Oh—he was gay with his front door, was he?" asked Perkins.

"He was thot, an' not ony too careful uv his windy-shades," replied Finn.

Perkins looked at him inquiringly.

"Givin' me, Mike Finn, song an' dance about not bein' home, wid me fri'nds outside on the lawn watchin' him troo de windy, laffin' loike a hayeny."

"Excuse me—like a what?" said Thaddeus.

"A hayeny," repeated Mr. Finn. "Wan o' thim woild bastes as laffs at nothin' much. 'Is he home?' sez oi. 'Are yees a pershonal fri'nd?' says the gurl. 'Oi'm not,' sez oi. 'He ain't home,' says the gurl. 'Whin'll he be back?' says oi. 'Niver,' says she, shlammin' the dure in me face; and Mike Finn wid a certifikut uv election for um in his pocket!"

"A certificate of election?" cried Perkins. "And he wouldn't see you?"

"He would not."

"You were to an extent the balance of power, then?"

"That's what oi was," said Finn, enjoying what he thought was Perkins's dismay; for he knew well enough to whom he was talking. "Oi was the rale bonyfiday balance uv power. Oi've got foive sons, sorr, and ivery wan o' thim byes is conthracthors, or, what's as good, bosses uv gangs on public an' proivate works. There ain't wan uv thim foive byes as don't conthrol twinty-foive votes, an' there ain't wan uv 'em as don't moind what the ould mon says to um. Not wan, sorr. An' they resints the turnin' down uv their father."

"That's as it should be," said Perkins.

"An' ut's as ut was, me young fri'nd. Whin oi wint home to me pershonal fri'nds at th' Finn Club, Misther Perkins had losht me. Wan gone. Whin oi tould the Finn Club, wan hundred sthrong, he losht thim. Wan hundred and wan gone. Whin oi tould th' byes, he losht thim. Wan hundred an' six gone. An' whin they tould their twinty-foive apiece, ivery twinty-foive o' thim wint. Wan hundred an' six plus wan hundred an' twinty-foive makes two hundred an' thirty-wan votes losht at the shlammin' uv the front dure. An' whin two hundred an' thirty-wan votes laves wan soide minus an' the other soide plus, th' gineral result is a difference uv twoice two hundred an' thirty-wan, or foor hundred an' sixty-two. D'ye mind thot, sorr?"

"I see," said Perkins. "And as this—ah—this particular candidate was beaten by a bare majority of two or three hundred votes—"

"It was *me* as done it!" put in the balance of power, shaking his finger at Perkins impressively. "Me—Mike Finn!"

"Well, I hope Mr. Perkins hears of it, Mr. Finn," put in Thaddeus. "I am told that he is wondering yet what hit him, and having put the affront upon you, and through that inexcusable act lost the election, he ought to know that you were his Nemesis."

"His what?" queried the real balance.

"His Nemesis. Nemesis is the name of a Greek goddess," exclaimed Perkins.

"Oi'm no Greek, nor no goddess," retorted Finn, "but I give him the throw-down."

"That's what I meant," explained Thaddeus. "The word has become part of the English language. Nemesis was the Goddess of the Throw-down, and the word is used to signify that."

"Oh, oi see," said Finn, scratching his head reflectively. Perkins took his revelation a trifle too calmly. "You say you don't know this Perkins," he asked.

"Well, I never met him," said the ex-candidate, smiling. "But I know him."

Finn laughed again. "Oi'll bet ye do; an' oi guiss ye've seen his fa-ace long about shavin'-toime in the mornin' in the lukin'-glash—eh?"

"Well, yes," smiled Perkins. "I confess I'm the man, Mr. Finn; but now we are—personal friends—eh? I was fagged out that night, and—you didn't send in your card, you know—and I didn't know it was you." The balance of power cast down his eyes, and rubbing his hand on his overalls as if to clean it, stretched it out. Perkins grasped it, and Finn gave a slight gulp. He wasn't quite happy. The proffered friendship of the man he had helped to defeat rather upset him; but he was equal to the occasion.

"Niver moind, sorr," he said, when he had quite recovered. "You're young yit. They've shoved yees out this toime, but wait awhoile. Yees'll be back."

"No, Mr. Finn," replied Perkins, handing Finn a cigar. "Thanks to you, I got out of a tight hole, and as our maid said to you that night, I'll 'niver be back.' But if you happen down my way again, I'll be glad to see you—at any time. Good-bye."

The two parted, and Thaddeus walked home, thinking deeply of the far-reaching effect in this life of little things; and as for Finn, he bit off half the cigar Perkins had given him, and as he chewed upon it, sitting on the edge of his barrow, he remarked forcibly to himself, "Well, oi'll be daamned!"

# JARLEY'S EXPERIMENT

Jarley was an inventive genius. He invented things for the pleasure of it rather than with any idea of ultimately profiting from the results of his ingenuity, which may explain why it was that his friends deemed many of his contrivances a sheer waste of time. Among other things that Jarley invented was a tennis-racket which could be folded up and packed away in a trunk. The fact that any ordinary tennis-racket could be packed away in any ordinary trunk without being folded up was to Jarley no good reason why he should not devote his energies to the production of the compact weapon of sport which he called the Jarley Racket. He was after novelty, and utility was always a secondary consideration with him. Others of his inventions were somewhat more startling. "The Jarley Ready Writing-Desk for Night Use," for instance, was a really remarkable conception. Its chief value lay in the saving of gas and midnight oil to impecunious writers which its use was said to bring about, and when fully equipped consisted simply of a writing-table with all the appliances and conveniences thereof treated with phosphorus in such a manner that in the blackest of darkness they could all be seen readily. The ink even was phosphorescent. The paper was luminous in the dark. The penholders, pens, pen-wipers, mucilage-bottle, everything, in fact, that an author really needs for the production of literature, save ideas, were so prepared that they could not fail to be visible to the weakest eye in the darkest night without the aid of other illumination. The chief trouble with the invention was that in the long-run it was more expensive than gas or oil could possibly be in the most extravagant household; but that bothered Jarley not a jot. Nor was he at all upset when his ingenious Library Folding-Bed, comprising a real bookcase and sofa-couch, failed to suit his practical-minded friends because, when turned down for use as a couch, all the books in the bookcase side of it fell out upon the floor. His arrangement was better than the ordinary folding-bed, he said, because the bookcase side of it was not a sham, but the real thing, while that of the folding-bed of commerce was a delusion and a snare. As a hater of shams he justified his invention, though of course it couldn't be put to much practical use unless the purchaser was willing to take his books out of the shelves when he intended using the piece of furniture for sleeping purposes. If the purchaser was too lazy to do this it was not Jarley's fault, so the inventor reasoned, nor did he intend improving his machine in order to accommodate the lazy man in his pursuit of a life of indolence.

When Jarley married he turned his attention to the devising of apparatus to make domestic life less trying to Mrs. Jarley. As a bachelor he had contrived quite a number of mechanical effects which made his lonely life easier. He had fitted up his rooms with devices by means of which, while lying in bed on cold mornings, he could light his gas-stove without getting up; and his cigars, the ends of which he had dipped in sulphur, so that they could be lit by scratching them on the under side of the mantel-piece, just as matches are ignited, were the delight of his life. Now, however, he turned his mind towards helping little Mrs. Jarley on in the domestic world. He prepared a chart by means of which the monotony of marketing was done away with entirely. He also arranged for her a charming automatic curl-paper box, and drew up a plan for a patent pair of curling-tongs, which could be fastened to the gas-fixture and kept heated to the degree required, so that it might be used at a moment's notice. This was provided with a number of movable ends, all different, in order that Mrs. Jarley could, if she chose, vary the appearance of her curls according to her taste; and although the little lady never approved of it sufficiently to have it made, it was undoubtedly a valuable contrivance.

Then when Jarley junior came along to delight the parent soul, self-rocking cradles and perpetual reservoirs for food were devised, and some of them put into actual use, though, as a rule, Mrs. Jarley preferred the old-fashioned methods to which she was by her home training more accustomed.

The great invention of Jarley, however, was the result of his study of Jarley junior as that very charming and exceedingly agile child developed from infancy into boyhood. The idea came to him one Sunday afternoon while Mrs. Jarley was at church. It was the nursemaid's afternoon out, and Jarley had undertaken to care for Master Jarley in the absence of his true guardians.

"Well, Jack," he said to his son, when they had been left in sole possession of the Jarley mansion, "you and I must entertain each other this afternoon. What shall we do?"

"I'd like to play choo-choo car with you," said Jack. "I'll be the engine and you be the train."

"Very well," said Jarley. "Have you got your steam up?"

"Yeth," lisped Jack. "All aboard!"

Jarley hitched himself on to the engine as best he could by grabbing hold of Jack's little coat tail, and the train started. It was the most tedious journey Jarley ever undertook. The train went up and down stairs, out upon the piazza, and finally landed in the kitchen, where the engine fired up on such fuel as gingerbread and cookies. Incidentally the train, as represented by Jarley, took on a load of freight, consisting of the same fuel, and off they started again. At the end of a half-hour's run Jarley was worn out, but the engine seemed to gather strength and speed the farther it travelled; and as it let out a fearful shriek—possibly a whistle—every time the rear end of the train suggested side-tracking and a cessation of traffic for a month or two, Jarley in his indulgence invariably withdrew the proposition. The consequence was that when Mrs. Jarley returned from church Jarley was a wreck, and as he handed the engine over to the maternal care he observed with some testiness that in a well-kept household it seemed to him matters should be so arranged that a busy man should not be compelled to turn himself into a child's nurse, especially on the one day of the week which he could devote to rest and relaxation. "If I had that boy's energy," he said to himself as he fled to his library, "what wonders I would accomplish! What a shame it is, too, that the wasted energy of youth cannot be stored up in some way, so that when there comes the real need for it, it can be made available!"

This thought was the germ of his invention. As he lay there in the library he thought over the possibilities of life if the nervous force of childhood, the misdirected energy of play-time, could only be put by and drawn upon later just as man puts by the money he does not need in the present for use in case of future rainy days. Then, as the sun sank below the hills and the twilight hours with their inspiring softness came on, Jarley resolved that he was the man to whom had come the mission which should make of this ideal a reality. Probably in the full glare of day he would not have undertaken it; but Jarley, in common with most men of dreamy nature, felt in the quiet dusk the power to do all things. He had the poetic temperament which sometimes leads on to great things, and the man so gifted who does not feel himself capable, at that hour of the day of rest, of battering down Gibraltar or of upbuilding the whole human race, must account himself a failure.

"I'll do it," he murmured, drowsily, to himself, and he did. How he did it was Jarley's own secret, and while he confides many things to me, this secret he kept, and still keeps. All I know is that he fitted up a play-room for Jack on the attic floor, and by means of an apparatus, the peculiarities of whose construction he alone knows, he managed after a while to store up the superfluous energy which Jack expended upon everything that he did. Every time Jack turned a somersault he contributed, unknown to himself, something to the growing bulk of hoarded force in the reservoir provided for its reception. All the strength necessary for the somersault was devoted to that operation. The superfluity went to the reservoir. So, also, when in his play of scaling imaginary rocks after fictitious wild beasts he endeavored futilely to walk up the play-room wall, the unavailing energy went to augment the stores from which Jarley hoped to extract so much that would prove of value to the world.

When the reservoir was full the question that confronted Jarley was as to the value of its contents, and to ascertain this he resolved upon an experiment upon himself. No one else, he believed, would be willing to subject himself to the experiment, nor did he wish at that time to let others into his secret. Even Mrs. Jarley was not aware of his efforts, and so he made the experiment. He liquefied the energy Jack had wasted, and upon retiring one night took what he considered to be the proper dose for the test. The effect was remarkable.

When he rose up the next morning he experienced a consciousness of power that reminded him of sundry tales of Samson. But there was one drawback. He did not seem quite able to control himself. For instance, instead of dressing in the usual dignified and quiet way, he found himself prancing about his room like a young colt, and while he was taking his bath he had a yearning for objects of juvenile *virtu* which had for many years been strangers to his tub. He was not at all satisfied with his dip plain and unadorned, and he had developed an unconquerable aversion for soap. It was all he could do to restrain his inclination to call vociferously for a number of small tin boats and birch-bark canoes, without which Jack never bathed. He did conquer it, however, and at the end of a half-hour managed to reach the end of his bath, though as a rule he had hitherto rarely expended more than ten minutes in his morning ablutions. Then came another difficulty. He found himself utterly unable to stand still while he was putting on his clothes, and finally Mrs. Jarley had to be called in to comb his hair for him. Jarley himself could no more have taken the time to part it satisfactorily than he could have flown.

"What *is* the matter with you?" said Mrs. Jarley, as she made several ineffectual attempts to get his truant locks into shape. "Have you caught St. Vitus's dance?"

"Nothing's the matter with me," returned Jarley, standing on one foot and hopping up and down thereon. "I feel well, that's all."

And then he tore out of the room, mounted the banisters, and slid downstairs in an utterly unbecoming fashion, considering that he was a man of thirty-five and the head of the house. He felt a little ashamed of himself in the midst of this operation, particularly when he observed that the waitress was standing in the hall below-stairs, looking at him with eyes that betokened an astonishment as creditable to her as it was disgraceful to him. He tried vainly to stop his wild descent when he noted her presence. He clutched madly at the banisters, turning his hands and knees into brakes in his effort to save his dignity; but once started he could not stop, and as a consequence he went down like a flash, slid precipitately over the newel-post, and landed with a cry of mortification on the hall floor. He was not hurt, save in his self-esteem, and gathering himself together, he endeavored to walk with dignity into the dining-room; but he had hardly reached the door, when he was overcome with a mad desire to whoop—and whoop he did. As a consequence of the whoop Jack was scolded when Mrs. Jarley came down. She had no idea that Jarley himself could be so blind to propriety as to yell in so indecorous a fashion; and when poor little Jack was upbraided, Jarley, despite his good intention to confess himself the guilty party, discovered that the only act he was capable of was giggling. Jack of course wept, and the more he wept the more Jarley giggled, and was taken to task for encouraging the boy in his misbehavior.

During breakfast he was unusually demonstrative. He could not bring himself to await his turn when the potatoes were passed, and in his eagerness to get at them he overturned his coffee, which served to turn the tables a little, for Jack giggled at the mishap, while Jarley became the centre of Mrs. Jarley's displeasure. What was worse, Jarley, try as he might, could not resist the temptation to kick the legs of the table, and it was not until Mrs. Jarley had threatened to dismiss Jack from her presence, supposing that he must, of course, be the offender, that Jarley assumed the burden of his misbehavior.

It was not until Jarley set out to his office, however, that he realized the real horror of his condition. Instead of riding down-town on one cable-car, as was his wont, he found himself trying, boy-like, to steal a ride by jumping on a car platform and standing there until the conductor came along, when he would hop off, ride a block or two on the end of a truck, and then try a new car, so beating his way down-town. Then he arrived at his office. I have neglected to state that while invention was Jarley's avocation, he was by profession a lawyer, being the junior member of a highly successful firm, at the head of which was no less a person than the eminent William J. Baker, whose record at the bar is too well known to require any further words of mine to recall him to the minds of my readers. Jarley had not been in the office more than ten minutes before he realized that he might better have remained at home while the influence of Jack's wasted energy was within him. He was in a state of irrepressibility. No matter how strongly he endeavored to hold himself in check he could not do so, and his day down-town was like the days of most boys who are permitted to spend a morning and an afternoon with their parent in the workshop. The first thing he did on reaching his desk was to roll back its folding top. This pleased him unaccountably. He had never before imagined that so much fun could be got out of the rolling top of a desk, and for a full quarter of an hour he pulled it backward and forward, and so noisily withal that Mr. Baker sent one of the clerks in to see if the office-boy had not become suddenly insane.

Recalled to his true self for the moment, Jarley endeavored to get down to work, but as he made the endeavor he became conscious that a revolving chair has very pleasing qualities to one who is fond of twirling. Round and round he twirled, and as he twirled he grabbed up his cane, and in a moment realized that he was playing that he was on a merry-go-round, and trying to secure a renewal of his right to ride by catching imaginary rings on the end of his stick. This operation consumed quite five minutes more of his time, and was accompanied by such a vast number of "Hoop-las" that Mr. Baker came himself to see what was the cause of the unseemly racket. Fortunately for Jarley, just as his partner reached the doorway, the chair had reached the limit of its twirling capacity, and having been unscrewed as far as it could be, toppled over on to the floor, with Jarley underneath. "What in the world does this mean, Jarley?" said Mr. Baker, severely, as he assisted his fallen partner to rise.

"My chair has come apart," laughed Jarley, getting red in the face.

"That's the great trouble with that kind of chair," said Mr. Baker. "You don't seem to mind the mishap very much."

"Oh no," said Jarley, gritting his teeth in his determination not to follow his mad impulse to jump on Mr. Baker's shoulders and clamor for a picky-back ride. "No; I don't mind little things like that much."

Here he stood on his right leg, as he had done before breakfast, and began to hop.

"Hurt your foot?" queried Mr. Baker.

Jarley seized at the suggestion with all the despairing vigor of a drowning man clutching at a rope.

"Yes; a little, but not enough to mention," he said; whereupon, much to his relief, Mr. Baker turned away and went back to his own room.

"This will never do," Jarley moaned to himself when his partner had gone. "If one of my clients should come in—"

Then he stopped and grinned like a mischievous lad. He had caught sight of an old water-meter that had been used as an exhibit in a case he had once tried against the city in behalf of an inventor, who had been led to believe that the water board would adopt his patent and compel every householder to buy one for the registration of water consumed. What fun it would be to take that apart, he thought, and thinking thus was enough to set him about the task. He locked his door, moved the strange-looking contrivance out into the middle of the room, and tried to unscrew the top of it with his eraser. The delicate blade of this improvised screw-driver snapped off in an instant, whereupon Jarley tried the scissors, with similar results. After a half-hour of this he gave up the idea of taking the meter apart, but his soul immediately became possessed of another idea, which was to see if it worked. The pursuit of this brought him the most deliriously joyful sensations; and for an hour he devoted himself to filling the machine up with water drawn from a faucet at one side of his room, and poured into the meter from a drinking-glass. It was not until the hour was up that he observed that the water after passing through the meter came out upon the carpet, and it is probable that even then he would not have noticed it had not the tenants below sent up to inquire if there was not something wrong with the water-pipes overhead.

When Jarley realized what had happened he wisely determined to give up business for the day. While the spirit of Jack was within him, the business he might transact was not likely to prove of value to himself or to any one else. So he put on his hat and coat, called a cab, and started for home. His experiences in the cab were quite of a kind with the experiences of the morning, and attended with no little personal danger. He would lean against the cab door and put his arm out and try to touch horse-cars as they passed. Once or twice he nearly had his head knocked off by sticking it out of the windows; but by some happy chance he got interested in the cab curtains and the inviting little strings, which, when pulled, made them fly up with a snap. Absorbed in this occupation, he drove on, and gave up all such dangerous experiments as playing tag with horse-cars and trucks, and arrived at home in time for luncheon unhurt.

Mrs. Jarley was somewhat alarmed at the unexpected return of Mr. Jarley, but was content with his explanation that while he never felt better in his life, he deemed it best to return and attend to his work in the privacy of his own home. For the proper accomplishment of this work he said that he thought he would use Jack's nursery on the attic floor, where he could be quiet, and he asked as an especial favor that he might be left alone with Jack for the balance of the day.

He had made up his mind that his experiment, while a success in one way, were not what he expected in another way. He had found Jack's energy very energetic indeed, but not suited for adult use, and he even found himself wondering why he had not thought of that before. However, the thing to do now was to get rid of that spirit as soon as possible. If it had become permanently a part of him, he had reached his second childhood, which for a man of thirty-five is a disturbing thought. So disturbing was it that Jarley resolved upon a heroic measure to cure himself. *Similia similibus* struck him as being the only possible cure, and so, regardless of the possible consequences to his physical being, he "permitted" Jack to be with him up-stairs "while he worked," as he put it to Mrs. Jarley, though all others were forbidden to approach.

The result was as he had foreseen. Jack's energy in Jack, pure and unadulterated, had very little trouble in wearing out the diluted energy which his father had acquired from his superfluous stores, and night coming on found Jarley, after a three hours' steady circus with his son, in his normal condition mentally. But physically! What a poor wreck of a human system was his when the last bit of the boyish spirit was consumed! Had he worked at brick-laying for a week without rest Jarley could not have been more prostrated physically. But he was happy. His tests had proved that he could do certain things, but the results he had expected as to the value of those things were not what he had hoped for. At any rate, his experiment gave him greater sympathy with his boy than he had ever had before, and they have become great chums. The greatest disappointment of the whole affair is Jack's, who wonders why it is that he and his father have no more afternoon acrobatics such as they had in the play-room that day, but until he is a good many years older his father cannot tell him, for the boy could not in the present stage of his intellectual development understand him if he tried.

As for Mr. Baker and the people at the office, they were not at all astonished to hear the next day that Jarley was laid up, and would probably, not appear at the office again for a week, although they were a little surprised when they learned that his trouble was rheumatism, and not softening of the brain.

# JARLEY'S THANKSGIVING

Jarley was in a blue mood the night before Thanksgiving. Things hadn't gone quite to suit him during the year. He had lost two of his most profitable clients—men upon whom for two years previously he had been able to count for a steady income. It is true that he had lost them by winning their respective suits, and had made two strong friends by so doing; but, as he once put it to Mrs. Jarley, the worst position a man could possibly get himself into was that of one who is long on friends and short on income. He did not underestimate the value of friends, but he didn't want too many of them; because beyond a certain number they became luxuries rather than necessities, and his financial condition was such that he could not afford luxuries.

"I love them all," he said, "but I haven't money enough to entertain a quarter of them. The last time Billie Hicks was up here he smoked sixteen Invincible cigars. Now, I am very fond of Billie Hicks, but with cigars at twenty cents apiece I can't afford him more than one Sunday in a year. He's getting a little cold because I haven't asked him up since."

"Why don't you buy cheaper cigars? At our grocery store they have some very nice looking ones at two for five cents," suggested Mrs. Jarley.

"I don't wish to have to move out of the house," said Jarley.

Mrs. Jarley failed to see the connection.

"Very likely you don't," said Jarley; "but if I smoked one of your two-and-a-half-cent grocery cigars in this house, you'd see the point in a minute. If you will get me a yard of cotton cloth, and let me put it in the furnace fire, you'll get a fair idea of the kind of atmosphere we'd be breathing if I allowed a cigar like that to be lit within fifty feet of the front door."

"But you can get a good cigar for ten cents, can't you?" Mrs. Jarley asked. "Yes—very good," assented Jarley; "but Billie would probably smoke thirty-two of those, and carry three or four away with him in his pockets. I'd lose even more that way. It's a singular thing about friends. They have some conscience about Invincible cigars, but they'll take others by the handful."

Jarley was also somewhat blue upon this occasion because none of his inventions—the little things he thought out in his leisure moments, and out of some of which he had hoped to gain a deal of profit—had been successful. The public had refused to place any confidence whatsoever in his patent reversible spats, which, when turned inside out, could be made useful as galoches; and the beaux of New York actually rejected with scorn the celluloid chrysanthemum, which he had hoped would become a popular boutonnière because of its durability and cheapness. An impecunious young man with care could make one fifteen-cent chrysanthemum of the Jarley order last through a whole season, and it could be colored to suit the wearer's taste with the ordinary paint-boxes that children so delight in; but in spite of this the celluloid chrysanthemum was a distinct failure, and Jarley had had his trouble for his pains, to say nothing of the cost of the model. But worst of all the failures, because of the prospective losses its failure entailed, was the Jarley safety lightning razor. Its failure was not due to any lack of merit, for it certainly possessed much that was ingenious and commendable. The affair was not different in principle from a lawn-mower. Six little sharp blades set on a cylinder would revolve rapidly as the pretty machine was pushed up and down the cheek of the person shaving, and leave the face of that person as smooth as a piece of velvet; but in announcing it to the world its inventor had made the unfortunate statement that a child could use it with impunity, and some would-be smart person on a comic paper took it up and wrote an undeniably clever article on the futility of inventing a razor for children. The consequence was that the safety razor was laughed out of existence, and the additions to his residence which Jarley was going to pay for out of the proceeds had to be abandoned.

"I don't like a blue funk," he said, "and generally I can find something to be thankful for at this season; but I'm blest if this year, beyond the fact that we're all alive, I can see any cause for celebrating my thankfulness. I haven't enough of it to last ten minutes, much less a day, what with the positive failure of my inventions, the loss of income from what I once considered safe investments that have gone to the wall, and the reduction of my professional earnings, not to mention the fact that almost at the beginning of my professional year I am as tired physically and mentally as I ought to be at the finish."

"Oh, well, say you are thankful, anyhow," suggested Mrs. Jarley. "You will convince others that you are, and maybe, if you say it often enough, you will convince yourself of the fact."

"Thanks," said Jarley. "It's possibly a good suggestion, but I don't believe in pretending to be what I'm not. It might convince me that I am thankful for something, but I don't want to be convinced when I know I'm not."

Which shows, I think, how very blue Jarley was.

"There's one thing," he added, with a sigh of relief at the thought—"I'll have a day of rest to-morrow anyhow. I've bought Jack a football, and he can take it out on the tennis-court and play with it all day, with intervals for meals."

"Why did you do that?" asked Mrs. Jarley, with a gesture not so much of indignation as of disapproval. "I think football is such a brutal game; and if Jack has a football at his present age, when he's in college he'll want to play. I don't want to have my boy wearing his hair like a Comanche Indian, and coming home with broken ribs and dislocated limbs."

"We'll let the broken ribs of 1904 and the wig of the same period suffice for the evils of that year," retorted Jarley. "It's the present I'm looking after, not the future ten or twelve years removed. If Jack hasn't that football to-morrow he'll have me, and I've no desire in the present condition of my physical well-being to be used by him as a plaything. Deprived of the leathern ball, he might use me as a football instead, and I must rest. That's all there is about it. Besides, if he becomes an aspirant for football honors now it will be a good thing for him. He'll take care of himself and try to improve his physique if he once gets the notion in his head that he wants to go on a university eleven. I want my boy to learn to be a man, and the football ambition is likely to be a very useful aid in that direction. He knits reins very well with a spool and a pin now, and I think it's time he graduated in that art, unless the woman of the future, of whom we hear so much, is to take man's place to such an extent that the man will have to take up woman's work. If I thought the masculine tendency of our present-day girls was likely to go much further, I might consent to the effemination of Jack simply to secure his comfort as a married man of the future; but I don't think that, and in consequence Jack is going to be brought up as a boy, and not as a girl. The football goes."

This remark was another indication of Jarley's depression. He rarely combated Mrs. Jarley's ideas, and when he did, and with a certain air of irritation, it was invariably a sign of his low mental state.

"When you say that the football goes, do you mean that it stays?" queried Mrs. Jarley, who was a little tired herself, and could not, therefore, resist the temptation to indulge in a bit of innocent repartee.

"I do," said Jarley, shortly. "Goes is sometimes a synonym for stays. When I feel stronger I may invent a new language, which will have fewer absurdities than English as she is spoke."

And with this Jarley went to bed, and slept the sleep of the just man who is truly weary.

If he had foreseen the result of his football investment it is doubtful if his sleep would have been so tranquil—unless, perchance, he were fashioned after that rare pattern of mankind, Louis XVI. of France, who called for his six or seven course dinner with a mob of howling, bloodthirsty Parisians in his antechamber, and who on the eve of his execution slept well, despite his knowledge that within fifteen hours his head would in all probability be lopped off by the guillotine to gratify the lust for blood which was the chief characteristic of the promoters of the first French Republic.

At six on the morning of Thanksgiving Day Jarley was sleeping peacefully, but the youthful Jack was not. Thanksgiving Day was not a holiday in his eyes, but a day set apart for work, thanks to his father's indulgence in providing him with a football. He had gone to bed the night before with the ball hugged tightly to his breast; and along about ten o'clock, when Jarley himself had gone into the nursery to put that treasured good-night kiss upon the forehead of his sleeping boy, tired as he was and blue as he was, he had difficulty in repressing the laughter that manifested itself within him, for Jack lay prone, face upward, with the football under the small of his back, and seemingly as comfortable as though he were resting upon eider-down.

"That is certainly a characteristic football attitude," Jarley said, when Mrs. Jarley had come to see what had caused her husband's chuckle.

"Yes—and so good for the spine!" returned Mrs. Jarley.

The attitude was changed, but the ball was left where Jack would see it the first thing on awaking in the morning. At six, as I have said, Jarley was sleeping peacefully, but Jack was not. He had opened his eyes some minutes before, and on catching sight of his treasured football he began to grin. The grin grew wider and wider, until apparently it got too wide for the bed, and the boy leaped out of his couch upon the floor. The first thing he did was to pat the ball gently but firmly, very much as a kitten manifests its interest in a ball of yarn. Then his attentions to his new plaything grew more pronounced and vigorous, and within fifteen minutes it had been chased out of the nursery into the parental bedchamber. Still Jarley slept. Mrs. Jarley was merely half asleep. She tried to tell Jack to be quiet; but she was not quite wide awake enough to do so as forcibly as was necessary, and the result was that instead of abating his ardor, Jack plunged into his sport more vigorously than ever.

And then Jarley was awakened—and what an awakening it was! Not one of those peaceful comings-to that betoken the tranquil mind after a good rest, but a return to consciousness with every warlike tendency in his being aroused to the highest pitch. Jack had passed the ball with considerable momentum on to the mantel-piece, which sent it backward on the rebound to no less a feature than the nose of the slumbering Jarley.

"What the deuce was that?" cried Jarley, sitting up straight in bed. He had forgotten all about the football, and to his suddenly restored consciousness it seemed as if the ceiling must have fallen. Then he rubbed his nose, which still ached from the force of the impact between itself and the ball.

"It was the ball did it, papa," said Jack, meekly. "'Twasn't me."

In an instant Jarley was on the floor; and Jack, scenting trouble, incontinently fled. The parent was angry from the top of his head to the soles of his feet, but as the soles of his feet touched the floor his anger abated. After all, Jack hadn't meant to hurt him, and having witnessed several games of football, he knew how innately perverse an oval-shaped affair like the ball itself could be. Furthermore, there was Mrs. Jarley, who had disapproved of his purchase from the outset. If he wreaked vengeance upon poor little Jack for his unwitting offence, Jarley knew that he would in a measure weaken his position in the argument of the night before. So, instead of chastising Jack, as he really felt inclined to do, he picked up the ball, and repairing to the nursery, summoned the boy to him in his sweetest tones.

"Never mind, old chap," he said, as Jack appeared before him. "I know you didn't mean it; but you must play in here until it is time for you to go out. Papa is very sleepy, and you disturb him."

"All right," said Jack. "I'll play in here. I forgot."

Then Jarley patted Jack on the head, rubbed his nose again dubiously, for it still smarted from the effects of the blow it had sustained, and retired to his bed once more. If he fondly hoped to sleep again, he soon found that his hope was based upon a most shifting foundation, for the whoops and cries and noises of all sorts, vocal and otherwise, that emanated from the next room destroyed all possibility of his doing anything of the sort. At first the very evident enjoyment of his son and heir, as Jarley listened to his goings-on in the nursery, amused him more or less; but his quiet smile soon turned to one of blank dismay when he heard a thunderous roar from Jack, followed by a crash of glass. Again springing from his bed, Jarley rushed into the nursery.

"Well, what's happened now?" he asked.

Jack's under lip curved in the manner which betokens tears ready to be shed.

"Nun-nothing," he sobbed. "I was just k-kicking a goal, and that picture got in the way."

Jarley looked for the picture that had got in the way, and at once perceived that it would never get in the way again, since it was irretrievably ruined. However, he was not overcome by wrath over this incident, because the picture was not of any particular value. It was only a highly colored print of three cats in a basket, which had come with a Sunday newspaper, and had been cheaply framed and hung up in the nursery because Jack had so willed. On principle Jarley had to show a certain amount of displeasure over the accident, and he did as well as he could under the circumstances, and retired.

For a while Jack played quietly enough, and Jarley was just about dozing off into that delicious forty winks prior to getting up when shrieks from the second Jarley boy came from the nursery. This time Mrs. Jarley, with one or two expressions of natural impatience, deemed it her duty to interfere. Jarley, she reasoned, had a perfect right to spoil Jack if he pleased, but he had no right to permit Jack to do bodily injury to Tommy; and as Tommy was making the house echo and re-echo with his wails, she deemed it her duty to take a hand. Jarley meanwhile pretended to sleep. He was as wide awake as he ever was; but the atmosphere was not full of warmth, and upon this occasion, as well as upon many others, his conscience permitted him to overlook the shortcomings of his elder son, and to assume a somnolence which, while it was not real, certainly did conduce to the maintenance of his personal comfort. Mrs. Jarley, therefore, rose up in her wrath. It was merely a motherly wrath, however, and those of us who have had mothers will at once realize what that wrath amounted to. She repaired immediately to the nursery, and without knowing anything of the technical terms of the noble game of football, instinctively realized that Jack and Tommy were having a "scrimmage." That is to say, she was confronted with a structure made up as follows: basement, the ball; first story, Tommy, with his small and tender stomach placed directly over the ball; second story and roof, Jack, lying stomach upward and wiggling, his back accurately registered on Tommy's back, to the detriment and pain of Tommy.

"Get *up*, Jack!" Mrs. Jarley cried. "What on earth are you trying to do to Tommy? Do you want to kill him?"

"Nome," Jack replied, innocently. "He wanted to play football, and I'm letting him. He's Harvard and I'm Yale."

A smothered laugh from the adjoining room showed that Jarley was not so soundly sleeping that he could not hear what was going on. Tommy meanwhile continued to wail.

"Well, get up,—right away!" cried Mrs. Jarley. "I sha'n't have you abusing Tommy this way."

"Ain't abusin' him," retorted Jack, rising. "I was 'commodatin' him. He wanted to play. When I don't let him play I get scolded, and when I do let him I'm scolded. 'Pears to me you don't want me to do anything."

Thus Thanksgiving Day began, not altogether well, but equanimity was soon restored all around, and everything might have run smoothly from that time on had not a cold drizzling rain set in about breakfast-time. It was clearly to be an in-door day. And what a day it was!

At ten o'clock the football came into play again.

At eleven the score stood: one clock knocked off the mantel-piece in the library; three chandelier globes broken to bits; one plaster Barye bear destroyed by a low kick from the parlor floor; Tommy with his nose very nearly out of joint, thanks to a flying wedge represented by Jack; Mrs. Jarley's amiability in peril, and Jarley's irritability well developed.

At twelve the ball was confiscated, but restored at twelve-five for the sake of peace and quiet.

At one, dinner was served and eaten in moody silence, Jack having inadvertently punted the ball through the pantry, grazing the chignon of the waitress, and landing in the mayonnaise. It was not a happy dinner, and Jarley began to wish either that he had never been born or that all footballs were in Ballyhack, wherever that might be.

"If it would only clear off!" he moaned. "That boy needs a playground as big as the State of Texas anyhow, and here we are cooped up in the house, with a football added."

"We'll have to take it away from him," said Mrs. Jarley, "or else you'll have to take Jack up into the attic and play with him. I can't have everything in the house smashed."

"We'll compromise on Jack's going to the attic. I have no desire to play football," returned Jarley; and this was the plan agreed upon. It would have been a good plan if Jarley had expended some of his inventive genius upon some such game as football solitaire, and instructed Jack therein beforehand; but this he had not done, and the result was that at three o'clock Jarley found himself in the attic involved in a furious game, in which he represented variously Harvard, the goal, the goal-posts, the referee, and acting with too great frequency as understudy for the ball. What he was not, Jack was, and the worst part of it was that there was no tiring Jack. The longer he played, the better he liked it. The oftener Jarley's shins received kicks intended for the football, the louder he laughed. When Jarley, serving as a goal-post, stood at one end of the attic, Jarley junior, standing several yards away, often appeared to mistake him for two goal-posts, and to make an honest effort to kick the ball through him. Slowly the hours passed, until finally six o'clock struck, and Master Jack's supper was announced.

The day was over at last. Wearily Jarley dragged himself down the stairs and reckoned up the day's losses. In glass and bric-à-brac destroyed he was some twenty or thirty dollars out. In mayonnaise dressing lost at dinner through the untoward act of the football he was out one pleasurable sensation to his palate, and Jarley was one of those, to whom, that is a loss of an irreparable nature. In bodily estate he was practically a bankrupt. Had he bicycled all morning and played golf all the afternoon he could not have been half so weary. Had he been thrown from a horse flat upon an asphalt pavement he could not have been half so bruised; all of which Mrs. Jarley considerately noted, and with an effort recovered her amiability for her husband's sake, so that after eight o'clock, at which hour Jack retired to bed, a little rest was obtainable, and Jarley's equanimity was slowly restored.

"Well," said Mrs. Jarley, as they went up-stairs at eleven, "it hasn't been a very peaceful day, has it, dear?"

"Oh, that all depends on how you spell peace. If you spell it p-i-e-c-e, it's been full of pieces," returned Jarley, with a smile; "but I say, my dear, I want to modify my statement last night that I had nothing to be thankful for. I have discovered one great blessing."

"What's that—a football?" queried Mrs. Jarley.

"Not by ten thousand long shots!" cried Jarley. "No, indeed. It's this: I'm more thankful than I can express that Jack is not twins. If he had been, you'd have been a widow this evening."

# HARRY AND MAUDE AND I—ALSO JAMES

We both loved Maude deeply, and Maude loved us. We know that, because Maude told us so. She told Harry so one Sunday evening on the way home from church, and she told me so the following Saturday afternoon on the way to the matinée.

This was the cause of the dispute Harry and I had in the club corner that Saturday night. Harry and I are confidants, and neither of us has secrets that the other does not share, and so, of course, Maude's feeling towards each of us was fully revealed.

We did not quarrel over it, for Harry and I never quarrel. I want to quarrel, but it is a peculiar thing about me that I always want to quarrel with men named Harry, but never can quite do it. Harry is a name which, *per se*, arouses my ire, but which carries with it also the soothing qualities which dispel irritation.

This is a point for the philosopher, I think. Why is it that we cannot quarrel with some men bearing certain names, while with far better men bearing other names we are always at swords' points? Who ever quarrelled with a man who had so endeared himself to the world, for instance, that the world spoke of him as Jack, or Bob, or Willie? And who has not quarrelled with Georges and Ebenezers and Horaces *ad lib.*, and been glad to have had the chance?

But this is a thing apart. This time we have set out to tell that other story which is always mentioned but never told.

Maude loved us. That was the point upon which Harry and I agreed. We had her authority for it; but where we differed was, which of the two did she love the better?

Harry, of course, took his own side in the matter. He is a man of prejudice, and argues from sentiment rather than from conviction.

He said that on her way home from church a girl's thoughts are of necessity solemn, and her utterances are therefore, the solemn truth. He added that, in a matter of such importance as love, the conclusion reached after an hour or two of spiritual reflection and instruction, such as church in the evening inspires, is the true conclusion.

On the other hand, I maintained that human nature has something to do with women. Very little, of course, but still enough to make my point a good one. It is human nature for a girl to prefer matinées to Sunday evening services. This is sad, no doubt, but so are some other great truths. Maude, as a true type of girlhood, would naturally think more of the man who was taking her to a matinée than of the fellow who was escorting her home from church, therefore she loved me better than she did Harry, and he ought to have the sense to see it and withdraw.

Unfortunately, Harry is near-sighted in respect to arguments evolved by the mind of another, though in the perception of refinements in his own reasoning he has the eye of the eagle. "Love on the way to a matinée," he said, "is one part affection and nine parts enthusiasm."

"And love on the return from church is in all ten parts temporary aberration," I returned. "It is what you might call Seventh Day affection. Quiet, and no doubt sincere, but it is dissipated by the rising of the Monday sun. It is like our good resolutions on New Year's Day, which barely last over a fortnight. Some little word spoken by the rector may have aroused in her breast a spark of love for you, but one spark does not make a conflagration. Properly fanned it may develop into one, but in itself it is nothing more than a spark. Who can say that it was not pity that led Maude to speak so to you? Your necktie may have been disarranged without your knowing it, and at a time when she could not tell you of it. That sort of thing inspires pity, and you know as well as I do that pity and love are cousins, but cousins who never marry. You are favored, but not to the extent that I am."

"You argue well," returned Harry, "but you ignore the moon. In the solemn presence of the great orb of night no woman would swear falsely."

"You prick your argument with your point," I answered. "There were no extraneous arguments brought to bear on Maude when she confessed to me that she loved me. It was done in the cold light of day. There was no moon around to egg her on when she confessed her affection for me. I know the moon pretty well myself, and I know just what effect it has on truth. I have told falsehoods in the moonlight that I knew were falsehoods, and yet while Luna was looking on, no creature in the universe could have convinced me of their untruthfulness. The moon's rays have kissed the Blarney-stone, Harry. A moonlight truth is a noonday lie."

"Doesn't the genial warmth of the sun ever lead one from the path of truth?" queried Harry, satirical of manner.

"Yes," I answered. "But not in a horse-car with people treading on your feet."

"What has that to do with it?" Harry asked.

"It was on a Broadway car that Maude confessed," I answered.

Harry looked blue. His eyes said:

"Gad! How she must love you!" But his lips said: "Ho! Nonsense!"

"It is the truth," said I, seeing that Harry was weakening. "As we were waiting for the car to come along I said to her: 'Maude, I am not the man I ought to be, but I have one redeeming quality: I love you to distraction.'

"She was about to reply when the car came. We were requested to step lively. We did so, and the car started. Then as we stood in the crowded aisle of the car we spoke in enigmas.

"'Did you hear what I said, Maude?' I asked.

"'Yes,' said she, gazing softly out of the window, and a slight touch of red coming into her cheeks. 'Yes, I heard.'

"'And what is your reply?' I whispered.

"'So do I,' she answered, with a sigh."

Harry laughed, and so irritatingly that had his name been Thomas I should have struck him.

"What is the joke?" I asked.

"You won't think it's funny," Harry answered.

"Then it must be a poor joke," I retorted, a little nettled.

"Well, it's on you," he said. "You have simply shown me that Maude never told you she loved you. That's the joke."

I was speechless with wrath, but my eyes spoke. "How have I shown that?" they asked in my behalf.

"You say that you told Maude that *you* loved *her* to distraction. To which declaration she replied, 'So do I.' Where there is in that any avowal that *she* loves *you* I fail to see. She simply stated that she too loved herself to distraction, and I breathe again."

"Hair-splitting!" said I, wrathfully.

"No—side-splitting!" returned Harry, with a roar of laughter. "Now my declaration was very different from yours. It was made when Maude and I were walking home from church. It was about nine o'clock, and the streets were bathed in mellow moonlight. I declared myself because I could not help myself. I had no intention of doing so when I started out earlier in the evening, but the uplifting effect of the service of song at church, combined with the most romantic kind of a moon, forced me into it. I told her I was a struggler; that I was not yet able to support a wife; and that while I did not wish to ask any pledge from her, I could not resist telling her that I loved her with all my heart and soul."

*I* began to feel blue. "And what did she say?" I asked, a little hoarsely.

"She said she returned my affection."

I braced up. "Ha, ha, ha!" I laughed. "This time the joke is on you."

"I fail to see it," he said.

"Of course," I retorted. "It is not one of your jokes. But say, Harry, when you send a poem to a magazine and the editor doesn't want it, what does he do with it?"

"Returns it. Ah!"

The "ah" was a gasp.

"You are the hair-splitter this time," said he, ruefully.

"I am," said I. "I could effectually destroy a whole wig of hairs like that. If you are right in your reasoning as to Maude's love for me, I am right as regards her love for you. We are both splitting hairs in most unprofitable fashion."

"We are," said Harry, with a sigh.

"There is only one way to settle the matter."

"And that?"

"Let's call around there now and ask her."

"I am agreeable," said I.

"Often," said Harry, ringing for our coats.

In a few moments we were ready to depart; and as we stepped out into the night, whom should we run up against but that detestable Jimmie Brown!

"Whither away, boys?" he asked; in his usual bubblesome manner.

"We are going to make a call."

"Ah! Well, wait a minute, won't you? I have some news. I'm in great luck, and I want you fellows to join me in a health to the future Mrs. B."

"Engaged at last, eh, Brown?" said Harry.

I did not speak, for I felt a sudden and most depressing sinking of the heart.

"Yes," said Brown; and then he told us to whom.

It is not necessary to mention the lady's name. Suffice it to say that Harry and I both returned to our corner in the club, discarded our overcoats, and talked about two subjects.

The first was the weather.

The second, the fickleness of women.

Incidentally we agreed that there was something irritating about certain names, and on this occasion James excited our ire somewhat more than was normal.

But we did not lick James. We had too much regard for some one else to split a hair of his head.

---

# AN AFFINITIVE ROMANCE

## I

### MR. AUGUSTUS RICHARDS'S IDEAL

Mr. Augustus Richards was thirty years of age and unmarried. He could afford to marry, and he had admired many women, but none of them came up to his ideals. Miss Fotheringay, for instance, represented his notions as to what a woman should be physically, but intellectually he found her wofully below his required standard. She was tall and stately—Junoesque some people called her—but in her conversation she was decidedly flippant. She was interested in all the small things of life, but for the great ones she had no inclination. She preferred a dance with a callow youth to a chat with a man of learning. She worshipped artificial in-door life, but had no sympathy with nature. The country she abominated, and her ideas of rest consisted solely in a change of locality, which was why she went to Newport every summer, there to indulge in further routs and dances when she wearied of the routs and dances of New York.

Miss Patterson, on the other hand, represented to the fullest degree the intellectual standard Mr. Augustus Richards had set up for the winner of his affections. She was fond of poetry and of music. She was a student of letters, and a clever talker on almost all the arts and sciences in which Mr. Augustus Richards delighted. But, alas! physically she was not what he could admire. She was small and insignificant in appearance. She was pallid-faced, and, it must be confessed, extremely scant of locks; and the idea of marrying her was to Mr. Augustus Richards little short of preposterous. Others, there were, too, who attracted him in some measure, but who likewise repelled him in equal, if not greater measure.

What he wanted, Mrs. Augustus Richards to be was a composite of the best in the beautiful Miss Fotheringay, the intellectual Miss Patterson, the comfortably rich but extremely loud Miss Barrows, with a dash of the virtues of all the others thrown in.

For years he looked for such a one, but season after season passed away and the ideal failed to materialize, as unfortunately most ideals have a way of doing, and hither and yon Mr. Augustus Richards went unmarried, and, as society said, a hopelessly confirmed old bachelor—more's the pity.

# II

## MISS HENDERSON'S STANDARD

Miss Flora Henderson was born and bred in Boston, and, like Mr. Augustus Richards, had reached the age of thirty without having yielded to the allurements of matrimony. This was not because she had not had the opportunity, for opportunity she had had in greatest measure. She made her first appearance in society at the age of seventeen, and for every year since that interesting occasion she had averaged four proposals of marriage; and how many proposals that involved, every person who can multiply thirteen by four can easily discover. Society said she was stuck up, but she knew she wasn't. She did not reject men for the mere love of it. It was not vanity that led her to say no to so many adoring swains; it was simply the fact that not one in all the great number of would-be protectors represented her notions as to the style of man with whom she could be so happy that she would undertake the task of making him so.

Miles Dawson, for instance, was the kind of man that any ordinary girl would have snapped up the moment he declared himself. He had three safe-deposit boxes in town, and there was evidence in sight that he did not rent them for the purpose of keeping cigars in them. He had several horses and carriages. He was a regular attendant upon all the social functions of the season, and at many of them he appeared to enjoy himself hugely. At the musicals and purely literary entertainments, however, Miles Dawson always looked,

as he was, extremely bored. Once Miss Henderson had seen him yawn at a Shelley reading. He was, in short, of the earth earthy, or perhaps, to be more accurate, of the horse horsey. Intellectual pleasures were naught to him but fountains of ennui, and being a very honest, frank sort of a person, he took no pains to conceal the fact, and it ruined his chances with Miss Henderson, at whose feet he had more than once laid the contents of the deposit-boxes— figuratively, of course—as well as the use of his stables and himself. The fact that he looked like a Greek god did not influence her in the least; she knew he was by nature a far cry from anything Greek or godlike, and she would have none of him.

Had he had the mental qualities of Henry Webster, the famous scholar of Cambridge, it might have been different, but he hadn't these any more than Henry Webster had Dawson's Greek godliness of person.

As for Webster, he too had laid bare a heart full of affection before the cold gaze of Miss Flora Henderson, and with no more pleasing results to himself than had attended the suit of his handsome rival, as he had considered Dawson.

"I think I can make you happy," he had said, modestly. "We have many traits in common. We are both extremely fond of reading of the better sort. You would prove of inestimable service to me in the advancement of my ambition in letters, as well as in the educational world, and I think you would find me by nature responsive to every wish you could have. I am a lover of music, and so are you. We both delight in the study of art, and there is in us both that inherent love of nature which would make of this earth a very paradise for me were you to become my life's companion."

Then Miss Flora Henderson had looked upon his stern and extremely homely face, and had unconsciously even to herself glanced rapidly at his uncouth figure, and could not bring herself to answer yes. Here was the intellectual man, but his physical shortcomings forbade the utterance of the word which should make Henry Webster the happiest of men. Had he written his proposal he would have stood a better chance, though I doubt that in any event he could have succeeded. Then he could have stood at least as an abstract mentality, but the intrusion of his physical self destroyed all. She refused him, and he went back to his books, oppressed by an overwhelming sense of loneliness, from which he did not recover for one or two hours.

So it went with all the others. No man of all those who sought Miss Henderson's favor had the godlike grace of Miles Dawson, combined with the strong intellectuality of Henry Webster, with the added virtues of wealth and amiability, steadfastness of purpose, and all that. It seemed sometimes to Miss Flora Henderson, as it had often seemed to Mr. Augustus Richards, that the standard set was too high, and that an all-wise Providence was no longer sending the perfect being of the ideal into the world, if, indeed, He had ever done so.

Both the man and the woman were yearning, they came finally to believe, after the unattainable, but each was strong enough of character to do with nothing less excellent.

---

# III

## A GLANCE AT MISS FLORA HENDERSON HERSELF

But what sort of a woman was Miss Flora Henderson, it may be asked, that she should demand so much in the man with whom she should share the burdens of life? Surely one should be wellnigh perfect one's self to require so much of another—and I really think Miss Flora Henderson was so.

In the first place, she was tall and stately—Junoesque some people called her. She had an eye fit for all things. It was soft or hard, as one wished it. It was melting or fixed, according to the mood one would have her betray. She was never flippant, and while the small things of life interested her to an extent, much more absorbed was she in the great things which pertain to existence. Dance she could, and well, but she danced not to the exclusion of all other things. With dancing people she was a dancer full of the poetry of motion, and enjoying it openly and innocently. With a man of learning, however, she was equally at home as with the callow youth. With nature in her every mood was she in sympathy. She was fond of poetry and of music; indeed, to sum up her character in as few words as possible, she was everything that so critical a dreamer of the ideal as Mr. Augustus Richards could have wished for, nor was there one weak spot in the armor of her character at which he could cavil.

In short, Miss Flora Henderson, of Boston, was the ideal of whom Mr. Augustus Richards, of New York, dreamed.

---

## IV

### A BRIEF GLIMPSE OF MR. AUGUSTUS RICHARDS

And as Miss Flora Henderson represented in every way the ideal of Mr. Augustus Richards, so did he represent hers. He had the physical beauty of Miles Dawson, and was quite the equal of the latter in the matter of wealth. So many horses he had not, but he owned a sufficient number of them. He was not horse-mad, nor did he yawn over Shelley or despise aesthetic pleasures. In truth, in the pursuit of aesthetic delights he was as eager as Henry Webster. He was in all things the sort of man to whom our heroine of Boston would have been willing to intrust her hand and her heart.

---

## V

## CONCLUSION

But they never met.

And they lived happily ever after.

---

# MRS. UPTON'S DEVICE

# *A Tale of Match-Making*

## I

### THE RESOLVE

"For when two
Join in the same adventure, one perceives
Before the other how they ought to act."

—BRYANT.

Mrs. Upton had made up her mind that it must be, and that was the beginning of the end. The charming match-maker had not indulged her passion for making others happy, willy-nilly, for some time—not, in fact, since she had arranged the match between Marie Willoughby and Jack Hearst, which, as the world knows, resulted first in a marriage, and then, as the good lady had not foreseen, in a South Dakota divorce. This unfortunate termination to her well-meant efforts in behalf of the unhappy pair was a severe blow to Mrs. Upton. She had been for many years the busiest of match-makers, and seldom had she failed to bring about desirable results. In the homes of a large number of happy pairs her name was blessed for all that she had done, and until this no unhappy marriage had ever come from her efforts. One or two engagements of her designing had failed to eventuate, owing to complications over which she had no control, and with which she was in no way concerned; but that was merely one of the risks of the business in which she was engaged. The most expert artisan sometimes finds that he has made a failure of some cherished bit of work, but he does not cease to pursue his vocation because of that. So it was with Mrs. Upton, and when some of her plans went askew, and two young persons whom she had designed for each other chose to take two other young people into their hearts instead, she accepted the situation with a merely negative feeling of regret. But when she realized that it was she who had brought Marie Willoughby and Jack Hearst together, and had, beyond all question, made the match which resulted so unhappily, then was Mrs. Upton's regret and sorrow of so positive a nature that she practically renounced her chief occupation in life.

"I'll never, never, never, so long as I live, have anything more to do with bringing about marriages!" she cried, tearfully, to her husband, when that worthy gentleman showed her a despatch in the evening paper to the effect that Mr. and Mrs. Jack had invoked the Western courts to free them from a contract which had grown irksome to both. "I shall not even help the most despairing lover over a misunderstanding which may result in two broken hearts. I'm through. The very idea of Marie Willoughby and Johnny Hearst not being able to get along together is preposterous. Why, they were made for each other."

"I haven't a doubt of it," returned Upton, with whom it was a settled principle of life always to agree with his better half. "But sometimes there's a flaw in the workmanship, my dear, and while Marie may have been made for Jack, and Jack for Marie, it is just possible that the materials were not up to the specifications."

"Well, it's a burning shame, anyhow," said Mrs. Upton, "and I'll never make another match."

"That's good," said Upton. "I wouldn't—or, if I did, I'd see to it that it was a safety, instead of a fusee that burns fiercely for a minute and then goes out altogether. Stick to vestas."

"I don't know what you mean by vestas, but I'm through just the same," retorted Mrs. Upton; and she really was—for five years.

"Vestas are nice quiet matches that don't splurge and splutter. They give satisfaction to everybody. They burn evenly, and are altogether the swell thing in matches—and their heads don't fly off either," Upton explained.

"Well, I won't make even a vesta, you old goose," said Mrs. Upton, smiling faintly.

"You've made one, and it's a beauty," observed Upton, quietly, referring of course to their own case.

So, as I have said, Mrs. Upton forswore her match-making propensities for a period of five years, and people noting the fact marvelled greatly at her strength of character in keeping her hands out of matters in which they had once done such notable service. And it did indeed require much force of character in Mrs. Upton to hold herself aloof from the matrimonial ventures of others; for, although she was now a woman close upon forty, she had still the feelings of youth; she was fond of the society of young people, and had been for a long time the best-beloved chaperon in the community. It was hard for her to watch a growing romance and not help it along as she had done of yore; and many a time did her lips withhold the words that trembled upon them—words which would have furthered the fortunes of a worthy suitor to a waiting hand—but she had resolved, and there was the end of it.

It is history, however, that the strongest characters will at times falter and fall, and so it was with Mrs. Upton and her resolution finally. There came a time when the pressure was too strong to be resisted.

"I can't help it, Henry," she said, as she thought it all over, and saw wherein her duty lay. "We must bring Molly Meeker and Walter together. He is just the sort of a man for her; and if there is one thing he needs more than another to round out his character, it is a wife like Molly."

"Remember your oath, my dear," replied Upton.

"But this will be a vesta, Henry," smiled Mrs. Upton. "Walter and you are very much alike, and you said the other night that Molly reminded you of me —sometimes."

"That's true," said Upton. "She does—that's what I like about her—but, after all, she isn't you. A mill-pond might remind you at times of a great and beautiful lake, but it wouldn't be the lake, you know. I grant that Walter and I are alike as two peas, but I deny that Molly can hold a candle to you."

"Oh you!" snapped Mrs. Upton. "Haven't you got your eyes opened to my faults yet?"

"Yessum," said Upton. "They're great, and I couldn't get along without 'em, but I wouldn't stand them for five minutes if I'd married Molly Meeker instead of you. You'd better keep out of this.

Stick to your resolution. Let Molly choose her own husband, and Walter his wife. You never can tell how things are going to turn out. Why, I introduced Willie Timpkins to George Barker at the club one night last winter, feeling that there were two fellows who were designed by Providence for the old Damon and Pythias performance, and it wasn't ten minutes before they were quarrelling like a couple of cats, and every time they meet nowadays they have to be introduced all over again."

"I don't wonder at that at all," said Mrs. Upton. "Willie Timpkins is precisely the same kind of a person that George Barker is, and when they meet each other and realize that they are exactly alike, and see how sort of small and mean they really are, it destroys their self-love."

"I never saw it in that light before," said Upton, reflectively, "but I imagine you are right. There's lots in that. If a man really wrote down on paper his candid opinion of himself, he'd have a good case for slander against the publisher who printed it—I guess."

"I should think you'd have known better than to bring those two together, and under the circumstances I don't wonder they hate each other," said Mrs.

Upton.

"Sympathy ought to count for something," pleaded Upton. "Don't you think?"

"Of course," replied Mrs. Upton; "but a man wants to sympathize with the other fellow, not with himself. If you were a woman you'd understand that a little better. But to return to Molly and Walter—don't you think they really were made for each other?"

"No, I don't," said Upton. "I don't believe that anybody ever was made for anybody else. On that principle every baby that is born ought to be labelled: *Fragile. Please forward to Soandso.* This 'made-for-each-other' business makes me tired. It's predestination all over again, which is good enough for an express package, but doesn't go where souls are involved. Suppose that through some circumstance over which he has no control a Michigan man was made for a Russian girl—how the deuce is she to get him?"

"That's all nonsense, Henry," said Mrs. Upton, impatiently.

"I don't know why," observed Upton. "I can quite understand how a Michigan man might make a first-rate husband for a Russian girl. Your idea involves the notion of affinity, and if I know anything about affinities, they have to go chasing each other through the universe for cycle after cycle, in the hope of some day meeting—and it's all beastly nonsense. My affinity might be Delilah, and Samson's your beautiful self; but I'll tell you, on my own responsibility, that if I had caught Samson hanging about your father's house during my palmy days I'd have thrashed the life out of him, whether his hair was short or long, and don't you forget it, Mrs. Upton."

Mrs. Upton laughed heartily. "I've no doubt you could have done it, my dear Henry," said she. "I'd have helped you, anyhow. But affinities or not, we are placed here for a certain purpose—"

"I presume so," said Upton. "I haven't found out what it is, but I'm satisfied."

"Yes—and so am I. Now," continued Mrs. Upton, "I think that we all ought to help each other along. Whether I am your affinity or not, or whether you are mine—"

"I *am* yours—for keeps, too," said Upton. "I shall be just as attentive in heaven, where marriage is not recognized, as I am here, if I hang for it."

"Well—however that may be, we have this life to live, and we should go about it in the best way possible. Now I believe that Walter will be more of a man, will accomplish more in the end, if he marries Molly than he will as a bachelor, or if he married—Jennie Perkins, for instance, who is so much of a manly woman that she has no sympathy with either sex."

"Right!" said Upton.

"You like Walter, don't you, and want him to succeed?"

"I do."

"You realize that an unmarried physician hasn't more than half a chance?"

"Unfortunately yes," said Upton. "Though I don't agree that a man can cut your leg off more expertly or carry you through the measles more successfully just because he has happened to get married. As a matter of fact, when I have my leg cut off I want it to be done by a man who hasn't been kept awake all night by the squalling of his lately arrived son."

"Nevertheless," said Mrs. Upton, "society decrees that a doctor needs a wife to round him out. There's no disputing that fact—and it is perfectly proper. Bachelors may know all about the science of medicine, and make a fair showing in surgery, but it isn't until a man is married that he becomes the wholly successful practitioner who inspires confidence."

"I suppose it's so," said Upton. "No doubt of it. A man who has suffered always does do better—"

"Henry!" ejaculated Mrs. Upton, severely. "Remember this: I didn't marry you because I thought you were a cynic. Now Walter as a young physician needs a wife—"

"I suppose he's got to have somebody to confide professional secrets to," said Upton.

"That may be the reason for it," observed Mrs. Upton; "but whatever the reason, it is a fact. He needs a wife, and I propose that he shall have one; and it is very important that he should get the right one."

"Are you going to propose to the girl in his behalf?" queried Henry.

"No; but I think he's a man of sense, and I know Molly is. Now I propose to bring them together, and to throw them at each other's heads in such a way that they won't either of them guess that I am doing it—"

"Now, my dear," interrupted Upton, "don't! Don't try any throwing. You know as well as I do that no woman can throw straight. If you throw Molly Meeker at Walter's head—"

"I may strike his heart. Precisely!" said Mrs. Upton, triumphantly. "And that's all I want. Then we shall have a beautiful wedding," she added, with enthusiasm. "We'll give a little dinner on the 18th—a nice informal dinner.

We'll invite the Jacksons and the Peltons and Molly and Walter. They will meet, fall in love like sensible people, and there you are."

"I guess it's all right," said Upton, "though to fall in love sensibly isn't possible, my dear. What people who get married ought to do is to fall unreasonably, madly in love—"

But Mrs. Upton did not listen. She was already at her escritoire, writing the invitations for the little dinner.

## II

### A SUCCESSFUL CASE

"The pleasantest angling is to see the fish
...greedily devour the treacherous bait."
—*Much Ado about Nothing.*

The invitations to Mrs. Upton's little dinner were speedily despatched by the strategic maker of matches, and, to her great delight, were one and all accepted with commendable promptness, as dinner invitations are apt to be. The night came, and with it came also the unsuspecting young doctor and the equally unsuspicious Miss Meeker. Everything was charming. The Jacksons were pleased with the Peltons, and the Peltons were pleased with the Jacksons, and, best of all, Walter was pleased with Miss Meeker, while she was not wholly oblivious to his existence. She even quoted something he happened to say at the table, after the ladies had retired, leaving the men to their cigars, and had added that "*that* was the way she liked to hear a man talk"—all of which was very encouraging to the well-disposed spider who was weaving the web for these two particular flies. As for Bliss—Walter Bliss, M.D.—he was very much impressed; so much so, indeed, that as the men left their cigars to return to the ladies he managed to whisper into Upton's ear,

"Rather bright girl that, Henry."

"Very," said Upton. "Sensible, too. One of those bachelor girls who've got too much sense to think much about men. Pity, rather, in a way, too. She'd make a good wife, but, Lord save us! it would require an Alexander or a Napoleon to make love to her."

"Oh, I don't know," said Bliss, confidently. "If the right man came along

—"

"Of course; but there aren't many right men," said Upton. "I've no doubt there's somebody equal to the occasion somewhere, but with the population of the world at the present figures there's a billion chances to one she'll never meet him. What do you think of the financial situation, Walter? Pretty bad, eh?"

Thus did the astute Mr. Upton play the cards dealt out to him by his fairer half in this little game of hearts of her devising, and it is a certain fact that he played them well, for the interjection of a more or less political phase into their discussion rather whetted than otherwise the desire of Dr. Bliss to talk about Miss Meeker.

"Oh, hang the financial situation! Where does she live, Henry?" was Bliss's answer, from which Upton deduced that all was going well.

That his deductions were correct was speedily shown, for it was not many days before Mrs. Upton, with a radiant face, handed Upton a note from Walter asking her if she would not act as chaperon for a little sail on the Sound upon his sloop. He thought a small party of four, consisting of herself and Henry, Miss Meeker and himself, could have a jolly afternoon and evening of it, dining on board in true picnic fashion, and returning to earth in the moonlight.

"How do you like that, my lord?" she inquired, her eyes beaming with delight.

"Dreadful!" said Henry. "Got to the moonlight stage already—poor Bliss!"

"Poor Bliss indeed," retorted Mrs. Upton. "Blissful Bliss, you ought to call him. Shall we go?"

"Shall we go?" echoed Upton. "If I fell off the middle of Brooklyn Bridge, would I land in the water?"

"I don't know," laughed Mrs. Upton. "You might drop into the smoke-stack of a ferry-boat."

"Of course we'll go," said Upton. "I'd go yachting with my worst enemy."

"Very well. I'll accept," said Mrs. Upton, and she did. The sail was a great success, and everything went exactly as the skilful match-maker had wished. Bliss looked well in his yachting suit. The appointments of the yacht were perfect. The afternoon was fine, the supper entrancing, and the moonlight irresistible. Miss Meeker was duly impressed, and as for the doctor, as Upton put it, he was "going down for the third time."

"If you aren't serious in this match, my dear, throw him a rope," he pleaded, in his friend's behalf.

"He wouldn't avail himself of it if I did," said Mrs. Upton. "He wants to drown—and I fancy Molly wants him to, too, because I can't get her to mention his name any more."

"Is that a sign?" asked Upton.

"Indeed yes; if she talked about him all the time I should be afraid she wasn't quite as deeply in love as I want her to be. She's only a woman, you know, Henry. If she were a man, it would be different."

The indications were verified by the results. August came, and Mrs. Upton invited Miss Meeker to spend the month at the Uptons' summer cottage at Skirton, and Bliss was asked up for "a day or two" while she was there.

"Isn't it a little dangerous, my dear?" Upton asked, when his wife asked him to extend the hospitality of the cottage to Bliss. "I should think twice before asking Walter to come."

"How absurd you are!" retorted the match-maker. "What earthly objection can there be?"

"No objection at all," returned Upton, "but it may destroy all your good work. It will be a terrible test for Walter, I am afraid—breakfast, for instance, is a fearful ordeal for most men. They are so apt to be at their very worst at breakfast, and it might happen that Walter could not stand the strain upon him through a series of them. Then Molly may not look well in the mornings. How is that? Is she like you—always at her best?"

Mrs. Upton replied with a smile. It was evident that she did not consider the danger very great.

"They might as well get used to seeing each other at breakfast," she said. "If they find they don't admire each other at that time, it is just as well they should know it in advance."

Hence it was, as I have said, that Bliss was invited to Skirton for a day or two. And the day or two, in the most natural way in the world, lengthened out into a week or two. There were walks and talks; there were drives and long horseback rides along shaded mountain roads, and when it rained there were mornings in the music-room together. Bliss was good-natured at breakfast, and Molly developed a capacity for appearing to advantage at that trying meal that aroused Upton's highest regard; and finally—well, finally Miss Molly Meeker whispered something into Mrs. Upton's ear, at which the latter was so overjoyed that she nearly hugged her young friend to death.

"Here, my dear, look out," remonstrated Upton, who happened to be present. "Don't take it all. Perhaps she wants to live long enough to whisper something to me."

"I do," said Molly, and then she announced her engagement to Walter Bliss; and she did it so sweetly that Upton had all he could do to keep from manifesting his approval after the fashion adopted by his wife.

"I wish I was a literary man," said Upton to his wife the next day, when they were talking over the situation. "If I knew how to write I'd make a fortune, I believe, just following up the little romances that you plan."

"Oh, nonsense, Henry," replied Mrs. Upton. "I don't plan any romances—I select certain people for each other and bring them together, that is all."

"And push 'em along—prod 'em slightly when they don't seem to get started, eh?" insinuated Upton.

"Well, yes—sometimes."

"And what else does a novelist do? He picks out two people, brings them together, and pushes them along through as many chapters as he needs for his book," said Henry. "That's all. Now if I could follow your couples I'd have a tremendous advantage in basing my studies on living models instead of having to imagine my realism. I repeat I wish I could write. This little romance of Mollie and Walter that has just ended—"

"Just what?" asked Mrs. Upton.

"Just ended," repeated Upton. "What's the matter with that?"

"You mean just begun," said Mrs. Upton, with a sigh. "The hardest work a match-maker has is in conducting the campaign after the nominations are made. When two people love each other madly, they are apt to do a great deal of quarrelling over absolutely nothing, and I'm not at all sure that an engagement means marriage until the ceremony has taken place."

"And even then," suggested Henry, "there are the divorce courts, eh?"

"We won't refer to them," said Mrs.

Upton, severely; "they are relics of barbarism. But as for the ending of my romance, my real work now begins. I must watch those two young people carefully and see that their little quarrels are smoothed over, their irritations allayed, and that every possible difference between them is adjusted."

"But you and I didn't quarrel when we were engaged," persisted Upton.

"No, we didn't, Henry," replied Mrs. Upton. "But that was only because it takes two to make a quarrel, and I loved you so much that I was really blind to all your possibilities as an irritant."

"Oh!" said Henry, reflectively.

---

## III

### A SET-BACK

"All is confounded, all!
Reproach and everlasting shame
Sits mocking in our plumes."
—*Henry V.*

Time demonstrated with great effectiveness the unhappy fact that Mrs. Upton knew whereof she spoke when she likened an engagement to a political campaign, in that the real battle begins after the nominations are made. Walter Bliss had decided views as to life, and Miss Meeker was hardly less settled in her convictions. Long before she had met Bliss, in default of a real she had builded up in her mind an ideal man, which at first, second, and even third sight Walter had seemed to her to represent. But unfortunately there is a fourth sight, and the lover or the *fiancée* who can get beyond this is safe— comparatively safe, that is, for everything in this world has its merits or its demerits, comparatively speaking, and the comparison is more often than not made from the point of view of what ought to be rather than of what really is. Mrs. Upton was a realist—that is, she thought she was; and so was Miss Meeker. Everybody looks at life from his or her own point of view, and there must always be, consequently, two points of view, for there will always be a male way and a female way of looking at things. Walter was in love with his profession. Molly was in love with him as an abstract thing. She knew nothing of him as a Washington fighting measles; she was not aware whether he could combat tonsillitis as successfully as Napoleon fought the Austrians or not, and it may be added that she didn't care. He was merely a man in her estimation; a thing in the abstract, and a most charming thing on the whole. He, on the other hand, looked upon her not as a woman, but as a soul, and a purified soul at that: an angel, indeed, without the incumbrance of wings, was she, and with a rather more comprehensive knowledge of dress than is attributed to most of angels. But two people cannot go on forming an ideal of each other continuously without at some time reaching a point of divergence, and Walter and Molly reached that point within ten weeks. It happened that while calling upon her one evening Walter received a professional summons which he admitted was all nonsense—why should people call in doctors when

119

it is "all nonsense"?

The call came while Walter was turning over the leaves at the piano as Molly played.

"What is this?" he said, as he opened the note that was addressed to him. "Humph! Mrs. Hubbard's boy is sick—"

"Must you go?" Molly asked.

"I suppose so," said Walter. "I saw him this afternoon, and there is not the slightest thing the matter with him, but I must go."

"Why?" asked Molly. "Are you the kind of doctor they call in when there's nothing the matter?"

She did not mean to be sarcastic, but she seemed to be, and Walter, of course, like a properly sensitive soul, was hurt.

"I must go," he said, positively, ignoring the thrust.

"But you say there is nothing the matter with the boy," suggested Molly.

"I'm going just the same," said Walter, and he went.

Molly played on at the piano until she heard the front door slam, and then she rose up and went to the window. Walter had gone and was out of sight. Then, sad to say, she became philosophical. It doesn't really pay for girls to become philosophical, but Molly did not know that, and she began a course of reasoning.

"He knows he isn't needed, but he goes," she said to herself, as she gazed dejectedly out of the window at the gaslamps on the other side of the street. "And he will of course charge the Hubbards for his services, admitting, however, that his services are nothing. That is not conscientious—it is not professional. He is not practising for the love of his profession, but for the love of money. I am disappointed in him—and we were having such a pleasant time, too!"

So she ran on as she sat there in the window-seat looking out upon the dreary street; and you may be sure that the commingling of her ideals and her disappointments and her sense of loneliness did not help Walter's case in the least, and that when they met the next time her manner towards him was what some persons term "sniffy," which was a manner Walter could not and would not abide. Hence a marked coolness arose between the two, which by degrees became so intensified that at about the time when Mrs. Upton was expected to be called in to assist at a wedding, she was stunned by the information that "all was over between them."

"Just think of that, Henry," the good match-maker cried, wrathfully. "All is over between them, and Molly pretends she is glad of it."

"Made for each other too!" ejaculated Upton, with a mock air of sorrow. "What was the matter?"

"I can't make out exactly," observed Mrs. Upton. "Molly told me all about it, and it struck me as a merely silly lovers' quarrel, but she won't hear of a reconciliation. She says she finds she was mistaken in him. I wish you'd find out Walter's version of it."

"I respectfully refuse, my dear Mrs. Upton," returned Henry. "I'm not a partner in your enterprise, and if you get a misfit couple returned on your hands it is your lookout, not mine. Pity, isn't it, that you can't manage matters like a tailor? Suit of clothes is made for me, I try it on, don't like it, send it back and have it changed to fit. If you could make a few alterations now in Molly—"

"Henry, you are flippant," asserted Mrs. Upton. "There's nothing the matter with Molly—not the least little thing; and Walter ought to be ashamed of himself to give her up, and I'm going to see that he doesn't. I believe a law ought to be made, anyhow, requiring engaged persons who want to break off to go into court and show cause why they shouldn't be enjoined from so doing."

"A sort of antenuptial divorce law, eh?" suggested Upton. "That's not a bad idea; you ought to write to the papers and suggest it—using your maiden name, of course, not mine."

"If you would only find out from Walter what he's mad at, and tell him he's an idiot and a heartless thing, maybe we could smooth it out, because I know that 'way down in her soul Molly loves him."

"Very well, I'll do it," said Upton, good-naturedly; "but mind you it's only to oblige you, and if Bliss throws me out of the club window for meddling in his affairs, it will be your fault."

The doctor did not quite throw Upton out of the window that afternoon when the subject came up, but he did the next thing to it. He turned upon him, and with much gravity remarked: "Upton, I'll talk politics, finance, medicine, surgery, literature, or neck-ties with you, but under no circumstances will I talk about woman with anybody. I prefer a topic concerning which it is possible occasionally to make an intelligent surmise at least. Woman is as comprehensible to a finite mind as chaos. Who's your tailor?"

"You ought to have seen us when he said that," observed Upton to his wife, as he told her about the interview at dinner that evening. "He was as solemn as an Alp, and apparently as immovable as the Sphinx; and as for me, I simply withered on my stalk and crumbled away into dust. Wherefore, my love, I am through; and hereafter if you are going to make matches for my friends and need outside help, get a hired man to help you. I'm did. If I were you I'd let 'em go their own way, and if their lives are spoiled, why, your conscience is clear either way."

But Mrs. Upton had no sympathy with any such view as that. She had been so near to victory that she was not going to surrender now without one more charge. She tried a little sounding of Bliss herself, and finally asked him point-blank if he would take dinner with herself and Upton and Molly and make it up, and he declined absolutely; and it was just as well, for when Molly heard of it she asserted that she had no doubt it would have been a pleasant dinner, but that nothing could have induced her to go. She never wished to see Dr. Bliss again—not even professionally. Mrs. Upton was gradually becoming utterly discouraged. The only hopeful feature of the situation was that there were no "alternates" involved. Bliss was done forever with woman; Miss Meeker had never cared for any man but Walter. Time passed, and the lovers were adamant in their determination never to see each other again. Repeated efforts to bring them together failed, until Mrs. Upton was in despair. It is always darkest, however, just before dawn, and it finally happened that just as hopelessness was beginning to take hold of Mrs. Upton's heart her great device came to her.

# IV

## THE DEVICE

"Music arose with its voluptuous swell,
And all went merry as a marriage bell."
—*Childe Harold*.

"Henry," said Mrs. Upton, one cold January morning, a great light of possibilities dawning upon her troubled soul, "don't you want to take me to the opera next Saturday? Calvé is to sing in 'Cavalleria,' and I am very anxious to hear her again."

"I am sorry, but I can't," Upton answered. "I have an engagement with Bliss at the club on Saturday. We're going to take lunch and finish up our billiard tournament. I've got a lead of forty points."

"Oh! Well, then, get me two seats, and I'll take Molly," said the astute match-maker. "And never mind about their being aisle seats. I prefer them in the middle of the row, so that everybody won't be climbing over us when they go out and in."

"All right; I will," said Henry, and the seats were duly procured.

Saturday came, and Upton went to the club, according to his appointment with Walter; but Bliss was not there, nor had he sent any message of explanation. Upton waited until three o'clock, and still the doctor came not; and finally he left the club and sauntered up the Avenue to his house, calling down the while imprecations upon the absent Walter.

"Hang these doctors!" he said, viciously. "They seem to think professional engagements are the only ones worth keeping. Off in his game, I fancy. That's the milk in the cocoanut."

Five minutes later he entered his library, and was astonished to see Mrs. Upton there reading.

"Why, hullo! You here?" he said. "I thought you were at the opera."

"No, I didn't go," Mrs. Upton replied, with a smile.

"There seems to be something in the air that prevents people from keeping their engagements to-day. Bliss didn't turn up," said Henry. "What did you do with the tickets?"

"I sent Molly hers by messenger, and told her I'd join her at the opera-house," said Mrs. Upton, her face beaming. "Did you say Walter didn't go to the club?" she added, anxiously.

"Yes. He's a great fellow, he is! Got no more idea about sticking to an engagement than a cat," said Upton. "Afraid of my forty points, I imagine."

"Possibly; but maybe this will account for it," said Mrs. Upton, with a sigh of relief, which hardly seemed necessary under the circumstances, handing her husband a note.

"What's this?" asked Upton, scanning the address upon the envelope.

"A note—from Walter," Mrs. Upton replied. "Read it."

And Upton read as follows:

> "SATURDAY MORNING, *January*—,
> 189-.
>
> "MY DEAR MRS. UPTON,—
> I am sorry to hear that Henry is called away, but there are compensations. If I cannot take luncheon with him, it will give me the greatest pleasure to listen to Calvé in your company. I may be a trifle late, but I shall most certainly avail myself of your kind thought of me.
>
> "Yours faithfully,
>
> "WALTER BLISS."

"What the deuce is this?" asked Upton. "I called away? Who said I was called away?"

"I did," said Mrs. Upton, pursing her lips to keep from indulging in a smile. "As soon as you left this morning I wrote Walter a note, telling him that you had been hurriedly called to Philadelphia on business, and that you'd asked me to let him know, not having time to do it yourself. And I closed by saying that we had two seats for 'Cavalleria,' and that, as my expected guest had disappointed me, I hoped he might come in if he felt like it during the afternoon and hear Calvé. That's his answer. I enclosed him the ticket."

"So that—" said Upton, beginning to comprehend.

"So that Molly and Walter are at the opera together. Hemmed in on both sides, so that they can't escape, with the Intermezzo before them!" said Mrs. Upton, with an air of triumph which was beautiful to look upon.

"Well, you are a genius!" cried Upton, finding his wife's enthusiasm contagious. "I'm almost afraid of you!"

"And you don't think I did wrong to fib?" asked Mrs. Upton.

"Oh, as for that," said Upton, "all geniuses lie! An abnormal development in one direction always indicates an abnormal lack of development in another. Your bump of ingenuity has for the moment absorbed your bump of veracity; but I say, my dear, I wonder if they'll speak?"

"Speak?" echoed Mrs. Upton. "Speak? Why, of course they will! Everybody talks at the opera," she added, joyously.

An hour later the door-bell rang, and the maid announced Miss Meeker and Dr. Bliss. They entered radiant, and not in the least embarrassed.

"Why, how do you do?" said Upton, as calmly as though nothing had happened. "Didn't see you at the club," he added, with a sly wink at his wife.

"Thought you were out of town," said Bliss; and then he turned and glanced inquiringly at the lovely deceiver. But Mrs. Upton said nothing. She was otherwise engaged; for Molly, upon entering the room, had walked directly to her side, and throwing her arms about her neck, kissed her several times most affectionately.

"You dear old thing!" she whispered.

"Mrs.—Upton—I'm very much obliged to you for a very pleasant afternoon," stammered Bliss, recovering from his surprise, the true inwardness of the situation dawning upon him, "as well as for—a good many pleasant afternoons to come. I– ah—I didn't see—ah—Molly until I got seated."

"No," said Molly; "and if he could have gotten away without disturbing a lot of people, I think he'd have gone when he realized where he was. And he wouldn't speak until the Intermezzo was half through."

"Well, I tried hard not to even then," said Walter; "but somehow or other, when the Intermezzo got going, I couldn't help it, and—well, it's to be next month."

And so it was. The wedding took place six weeks later; and all through the service the organist played the Intermezzo in subdued tones, which some people thought rather peculiar—but then they were not aware of all the circumstances.